Kristy and the Missing Child

**Other books by
Ann M. Martin**

Ma and Pa Dracula
Yours Turly, Shirley
Ten Kids, No Pets
Slam Book
Just a Summer Romance
Missing Since Monday
With You and Without You
Me and Katie (the Pest)
Stage Fright
Bummer Summer

BABY-SITTERS LITTLE SISTER series
THE BABY-SITTERS CLUB series
(see back of the book for a complete listing)

Kristy and the Missing Child
Ann M. Martin

AN
APPLE
PAPERBACK

SCHOLASTIC INC.
New York Toronto London Auckland Sydney

The author gratefully acknowledges
Ellen Miles
for her help in
preparing this manuscript.

Cover art by Hodges Soileau

ISBN 0-590-44800-5

12 11 10 9 8 7 6 5 4 3 2 1   2 3 4 5 6 7/9

Printed in the U.S.A.   28

First Scholastic printing, May 1992

CHAPTER 1

"Atta boy, that's right, pitch 'er in there, atta boy — *yes!*" I yelled that last word. "All right!" I said. "That was definitely a strike. I think you're getting the idea, Jake."

"Really, Kristy?" he asked. "Am I *really* getting better?" He looked pleased.

"Absolutely," I said. "In fact, I think you'll be a good relief pitcher one of these days."

Jake beamed. Patsy and Laurel threw down their gloves (they'd been playing catch while Jake and I worked on his pitching) and ran to hug him. "Yea, Jake!" said Laurel.

"Yea!" echoed Patsy. She looked happy for Jake, but she also looked a little bewildered. "Kristy," she asked me, "what is a relief pitcher, anyway?"

"Silly," said Laurel. "Don't you know anything? The relief pitcher is the guy who makes it all better. Like when Mommy says, 'Oh,

1

what a relief!' when the plumber comes to fix a leak or something.''

I laughed. Laurel has a funny way of putting things. But in a way, she was right. A relief pitcher *is* the guy who makes it all better. He or she comes into the game when the starting pitcher can't hack it anymore and, hopefully, wins the game.

How do I know all this stuff? Well, because I love baseball. I have two older brothers, so I grew up learning about sports. And now I coach my own softball team! It's not exactly the Mets, but we have fun. Kristy's Krushers (that's the name of my team) is made up mostly of kids who are too young — or too scared — to try out for Little League. There are girls *and* boys on the team, and they range in age from two and a half (can you believe it?) to eight.

I love coaching, maybe because I love being around kids. I've known most of the kids on my team for quite a while — and not just as their coach. I've also spent a lot of time baby-sitting for many of them. I love to baby-sit almost as much as I love to play, or watch, or coach sports. I even started a club for baby-sitters — but more about that later.

Maybe I should introduce myself. You've probably already figured out my name, right? It's Kristy. Kristy Thomas. I'm thirteen years old and I'm in the eighth grade at Stoneybrook Middle School. Which is in, naturally, a town called Stoneybrook. In Connecticut. And that day I was baby-sitting for the Kuhn kids, who are on my team.

It was the first time I'd sat for the Kuhns. Until that day, I'd only known them through the team. Jake is a friend of a kid I *do* sit for a lot, Buddy Barrett. And Buddy was the one who asked the Kuhns to join the team. But until recently, I guess the Kuhns didn't need a sitter, because Mrs. Kuhn wasn't working. Mrs. Kuhn has a job now, though — and part of the reason she's working is because she and Mr. Kuhn have separated. Their divorce was just finalized a little while ago.

The kids seem to be handling things well. Jake, who's eight, has a good head on his shoulders. I think he's a terrific big brother to Laurel, who's six, and Patsy, who's only five. A big brother can be a big help when your family is splitting up. Believe me, I know.

I was lucky enough to have *two* big brothers when my dad walked out on my family. That was years ago. Charlie and Sam were great back then, and they're great now, even though they tease me unmercifully whenever they get the chance. Charlie's seventeen and Sam is fifteen. I also have a little brother named David Michael. He's seven, and he barely remembers

3

our father because he was only a baby when Dad left.

For a long time, that was my family. Mom, Charlie, Sam, David Michael, and me. Then Mom met this guy named Watson Brewer, and she married him. I wasn't crazy about him at first, even though he *is* a millionaire, but now I really like him. Watson had also been married once before, and he has two children, Karen (she's seven) and Andrew (he's four). They're both Krushers, too. They live with us every other weekend and for two weeks in the summer. The rest of the time they live with their mother and stepfather.

Aren't families *complicated* these days?

And I haven't even told you quite how complicated my family really is! See, after Mom married Watson and we moved into his house (which I hated at first because it was all the way across town from our old house and old neighborhood), the two of them decided to adopt a baby together. And that's how Emily Michelle came to live with us. She's two and a half, she was born in Vietnam, and she's about the cutest thing I've ever seen. She's also a handful, which is why Nannie, my grandmother, came to live with us, too. Besides the humans in our family, we've also got a dog, a cat, and two goldfish.

You're probably wondering how we all fit into one house. Well, there's plenty of room, because Watson's house is actually a mansion. Really! I wasn't kidding when I said he was a millionaire.

Anyway, we live together happily most of the time. Of course, we fight occasionally, like every family, but underneath it all, we love each other. I'm lucky to have such a neat family.

Jake and Laurel and Patsy are lucky, too, even though they may not feel lucky right now. They didn't want their parents to get a divorce, and I know they're hurting. But the good thing is that their parents are acting like civilized human beings while they go about dissolving their marriage. Although they are trying to work out custody of the kids (Mrs. Kuhn has custody for now, but Mr. Kuhn wants to get joint custody), they aren't bad-mouthing each other, and they haven't turned into nasty, hateful people. They are still friendly to each other, and they both care a lot about the kids.

How do I know all this? Well, some of it is stuff Mrs. Kuhn told me, and some of it I know from hearing other adults in the neighborhood talk (everybody likes the Kuhns, and they miss Mr. Kuhn now that he's moved to Texas), and some of it I can just tell by being with the kids. They seem as happy and as well-adjusted as ever.

There are rough spots, though.

For example, Jake had been pretty *un*happy when I first arrived at the Kuhns' that day. "Mom's so unfair," he said to me as soon as she'd pulled out of the driveway. "Dad wanted to take me all the way to Europe, and she won't let me go!"

"Wow!" I said. "To Europe? That's a pretty big trip!"

"That's what Mom said," replied Jake. "She said that it was too far, and that two weeks was too long for me to be out of school. But Dad says that without me his business trip is going to be boring, boring, boring."

"Well, I'm sure he'll take you somewhere else another time," I said. I couldn't believe that Jake had actually had the chance to go to Europe. When I was his age, the farthest *I'd* ever been was Stamford. (That's the closest city to Stoneybrook.)

"That's what Mom said," said Jake again, with a sigh. "She also said I'd have plenty of other birthdays."

"Birthdays?" I asked.

"Yeah," he said. "I'm going to be nine soon. I'm having this big Teenage Mutant Ninja Turtle birthday party. There's even going to be a real Turtle at it! But Dad can't come to it."

"Oh, will he still be in Europe?" I asked.

"Nope," said Jake. "He'll be back. But he has other stuff to do in Texas. He keeps trying to figure out how he can see me on a day *near* my birthday, but every time he makes a plan it gets messed up. I think his boss is really mean."

"That's too bad," I said. I thought of all the birthdays *I'd* spent missing my dad. Once in a while he'd remember to send me a card, but usually he forgot. At least Jake's dad was trying. "But I'm sure he'll do everything he can to see you around the time of your birthday."

"Yeah," answered Jake, looking sad. Then he started to tell me all about his party, and before long he was looking a lot less sad. In fact, he looked pretty excited and happy. " . . . and my friends are each going to get a mask to wear, with the name of their favorite Turtle on it. I get to be Donatello!" he finished, grinning.

"Terrific!"

"I just wish Dad could come," Jake said, wistfully. He couldn't seem to forget about that.

"Maybe he will," said Patsy. She'd been sitting nearby, playing with her Barbie Ferrari. "I saw Daddy yesterday, you know."

"Patsy, don't make up stories," said Laurel, who had joined us. "You didn't see Daddy. He lives in Dallas now."

"I'm *not* making up stories," said Patsy. "He was here. I didn't really see *him*, but I saw his car. Maybe he just came to Stoneybrook for the day." I could tell that she had no idea what "Dallas" meant. After all, she's only five.

"You saw his car?" asked Jake.

Patsy nodded.

"That's weird," said Jake. "Nobody has a car like Dad's. It's an old car called a T-Bird, and it's painted a special green color."

"And I *saw* it," said Patsy stoutly.

Jake and Laurel looked at each other and shook their heads. "No way," said Laurel. But she said it so that Patsy couldn't hear. I could tell she didn't want to get into a big argument about it.

That's when I decided to see if the kids wanted to practice their softball. I knew that once they got involved in pitching and catching and hitting, they'd forget about everything else for a while. And I was right. The rest of the afternoon flew by. We didn't talk about anything heavier than how to throw a curve ball, and it ended up being a really nice day. I was glad I'd had a chance to get to know the Kuhn kids *off* the softball field.

8

CHAPTER 2

"You? Failing home ec? I don't believe it," I said. I shook my head.

"Me either," said Mary Anne. "But just because I like to do needlework and knit, doesn't mean I can do all that other stuff. I can't *stand* sewing, and I can't cook the way Mrs. Ploof wants me to. What am I going to do?" she wailed.

Mary Anne Spier is my best friend. We've known each other practically forever, and even though we're opposites in many ways, we seem to have some kind of special chemistry that helps us stick together. That afternoon, we were sitting on Claudia Kishi's front lawn. Our club meetings are always at Claudia's house. Mary Anne and I had both gotten there early, and the sun felt so good that neither of us could even *think* of going inside to wait for everybody else. I picked a blade of grass, stuck it between my thumbs, and blew on it. It made a loud, honking noise, and Mary Anne giggled. She grabbed another piece of grass and blew. Her grass made a high, squeaky noise, and both of us giggled. We sat there for a while longer, trying out different pieces of grass. We didn't talk, but the silence felt fine. That's one of the great things about being with your best friend, if you know what I mean.

As she picked blades of grass and examined them, Mary Anne was probably thinking about how she was going to pull up her home-ec grade. And maybe, as a friend, I should have been trying to help her figure it out. But instead, I was thinking about the BSC. That's the Baby-sitters Club, of course. The one that was going to be meeting up in Claud's room in about ten minutes.

I love to think about the BSC. Why? Well, I guess because it was my idea, and it was one of the best ideas I ever had. I don't want to sound conceited, but it was. It's more than just a club; it's a successful business. And all the people in it are terrific. I don't know what I'd do without the BSC.

I think the club works so well because of the way we set it up. We meet on Mondays, Wednesdays, and Fridays from 5:30 to 6:00. Any parent who needs a sitter can call during that time, and they'll be sure to find one. Simple, right? Our clients think so. They are incredibly happy to have seven reliable sitters a phone call away. We hardly ever have to distribute flyers or advertise, since we have plenty of business. Many of our clients have been using our club for quite a while now, and we've gotten to know their kids pretty well. We keep up-to-date with what's going on with them by writing in and reading the club notebook, where all the members record the details of each job they go on.

Our club is organized so that everyone in it has a job to fill. I'm president, since the club was my idea. I have to admit that I *love* being president. I guess it satisfies the part of me that's kind of bossy. But it's not as if I order everybody around. We have equal say in any decisions.

Our vice-president is Claudia Kishi. As I said, we hold our meetings in her bedroom, which is why she gets to be vice-president. We meet in her room because she has her own phone with a private line — an essential ingredient to our club's success. Claudia is terrific. She's Japanese-American, as you might have guessed from her name, and she's totally gorgeous and exotic-looking, from her long black hair to her almond-shaped eyes to the tips of her gold lamé high-tops. Claud is a *wild* dresser. And not just in relation to me, either. (I wear jeans and a turtleneck most days.

Clothes aren't important to me.) Claudia is the first to spot — or even make up — new trends.

Claudia's a really talented artist. And art is a top priority with her, unlike schoolwork. Claud's smart, don't get me wrong. (Even if she isn't a bona fide *genius* like her older sister Janine.) But she just doesn't seem to care too much about her grades.

Luckily, Claud doesn't have a club job that requires good math skills. But her best friend Stacey McGill does. Stacey's our treasurer, and she's as good at math as Claud is at art. She keeps track of every penny we each earn, and she also collects dues and keeps a record of how much money we have in the treasury. Then she doles it out as needed, whether it's for transportation (we pay my brother to drive me to meetings, since I live so far away now), a pizza party, or some other special event. We also use the money to buy things for our Kid-Kits, which are boxes full of toys and games. We've decorated our Kid-Kits to look really cool, and kids we sit for are always thrilled when we bring them along.

It's easy to see why Claudia and Stacey are best friends. Like Claudia, Stacey loves to "shop till she drops." She is a very cool, very sophisticated dresser. She has blonde hair that she gets permed once in a while, pierced ears, and the biggest collection of nail-polish colors I've ever seen. It's almost as if Stacey can't *help* being sophisticated; she grew up in New York City, the Big Apple. I think she's on a different level from the rest of us Stoneybrook girls.

But Stacey's life hasn't been easy. First of all, she's moved a few times in the last few years: once because her Dad got a job in Stoneybrook (that's when she first moved here), once because he got transferred back to New York City, and once because her parents got a divorce and Stacey and her mom returned to Stoneybrook. It's enough to make you dizzy! But Stacey has handled it well.

There's something else she handles well: her diabetes. Stacey has a pretty severe form of the disease, and she really has to take care of herself. Having diabetes means that her body doesn't make this stuff called insulin, which most of our bodies use all the time in order to process sugar and carbohydrates. So Stacey has to a) be very, very careful about what she eats (*no* sweets!) and b) give herself shots of insulin every single day. I don't know how she does it. I'm sure I'd be whining and complaining all the time, but you never hear a peep out of Stacey. In a way, I think having diabetes has made her more mature than the rest of us.

Our club's secretary is — guess who — my

best friend Mary Anne. Her job is to keep track of every appointment we line up: where it is, when it is, who has the job — everything. The record book she keeps is incredibly neat and organized, like Mary Anne herself. She *has* to be organized, since her position requires her to keep track of our schedules and let us know which of us is free for which jobs.

Besides being organized, Mary Anne is sensitive (she cries easily), romantic (she's the only one in our club who has a steady boyfriend), and shy. You've probably already figured out that I am *none* of those things —that's what I meant about us being opposites. But we're alike in some ways, too: We're both pretty short for our age, we both have brown hair and brown eyes, and we're both very loyal friends.

In fact, Mary Anne is a loyal *best* friend to two people — me and another girl in our club, Dawn Schafer. Actually, Mary Anne and Dawn are more than best friends. They're stepsisters! See, Mary Anne's father was a widower for a very long time, since her mother died soon after Mary Anne was born. Mr. Spier did his best to raise Mary Anne by himself. He did a pretty good job, too, except that he went a little overboard in the rules department. Mary Anne was still being treated like a fourth-grader when she was in seventh grade, as far as curfews and clothes and things like that.

Anyway, by the time Mary Anne was older, Mr. Spier started to relax a little. Maybe it was because he fell in love. The woman he fell in love with was Dawn's mother, who had actually been an old flame of Mr. Spier's way back in high school. She'd lived in California for a long time, where she'd gotten married, had two kids, and then gotten divorced. When she moved back to Stoneybrook, they clicked again, and the rest is history.

One of Mrs. Schafer's two kids is Dawn, our club's alternate officer. (The other is Jeff, Dawn's younger brother.) What's an alternate officer? Well, it's like a substitute teacher. If any member can't make it to a meeting, Dawn is prepared to do her job.

We call Dawn our California girl, since that's where she came from. Dawn has long blonde hair, blue eyes, a laid-back personality, and casual clothes. No matter how long she lives in Stoneybrook, Dawn will probably always wish she were on a beach, looking at the Pacific Ocean. Dawn's a real individual. She eats health food while the rest of us (except Stacey) eat junk, she has *two* holes pierced in each ear, and doesn't care what anybody else thinks of her. I know I'll never be that cool!

I think Dawn is pretty happy these days,

with Mary Anne and her father settled in at the old Schafer house (and I mean *old* —it even has a secret passageway that might be haunted!). But there's one thing that's hard for her, and that's how much she misses her brother Jeff. He just never adjusted to Stoneybrook, and he missed his dad like crazy, so it was decided that he should go back to California to live. Poor Dawn. I can't imagine how I'd feel if David Michael lived 3,000 miles away!

Claudia, Stacey, Mary Anne, Dawn, and I are all thirteen and in the eighth grade. But the two other members of our club are younger. Jessi Ramsey and Mallory Pike are both eleven and in the sixth grade. They're best friends. They are also our junior officers, which basically means that they aren't allowed to sit at night for anyone except their own families. This rule was made by their parents, but it's one rule that we can all live with. Jessi and Mal get *plenty* of afternoon business, so they're happy. And since they take those jobs they free the rest of us for nighttime sitting. So we're happy, too.

Mal is someone we used to sit for. She's the oldest in a family of eight kids! She's a terrific sitter, since she's had so much practice. She has curly red hair, glasses, and braces. She'd love to wear contacts, but her parents say she's too young. Mal loves to read, and she also loves to write. Someday she wants to write and illustrate kids' books!

Jessi also loves to read, but she has other ambitions. She wants to be a ballet dancer, and she's already well on her way. She takes a zillion dance classes, and she's extremely talented. Jessi's family is much smaller than Mal's; she has one younger sister and a baby brother. The Ramseys are one of the few black families in Stoneybrook, by the way. When Jessi first moved here, that fact made her life a little rough. Not everybody was ready to accept her family — just because of their color. But now the Ramseys are part of the community.

There are two other club members I haven't told you about: our associate members. They don't come to meetings, but they're ready and willing to take on jobs we can't cover. One of them is Shannon Kilbourne, a girl from my neighborhood. The other is a boy named Logan Bruno. Remember I told you that Mary Anne is the only club member with a steady boyfriend? Well, Logan's the one. He's a great guy.

I'd been thinking so hard about the BSC and its members that I was in kind of a fog. But suddenly I heard a wild honking and screeching coming from all around me. I looked up to see that Jessi, Mal, Claudia, Stacey, and Dawn had joined me and Mary Anne on the lawn — and each of them was blowing on a blade of grass! They sounded like some kind of crazy orchestra. I cracked up. Then I held up my hands and started to conduct them. When they finished their "symphony," we rolled around laughing for a few minutes until I glanced at my watch and realized it was nearly five-thirty.

We raced upstairs, just in time to hear the phone in Claud's room ring. I grabbed it. "Baby-sitter's Club!" I said, panting. "Can I help you?"

That was the first of many calls that afternoon, but between calls, we managed to talk a lot. Mary Anne told us about her awful home-ec class. I told everybody about the big practice game the Krushers would be having the next day, against Bart's Bashers. (Bart is this guy I like. He's the coach of my team's main rivals. I wouldn't exactly call him my *boyfriend*, but, well, you know.) We also talked a lot about the Awards Night that was going to take place soon. It's a tradition at SMS for eighth-graders to put on a program for themselves, and give out silly awards to each other. We were really looking forward to it.

"I just hope I don't get voted 'Most Often Seen Daydreaming,' or something," said Mary

Anne. "I would *die* if I had to go up on stage to accept a prize."

"I'd love to win 'Coolest Dresser,' but I bet you'll get that one," said Stacey to Claud.

"You never know," I said. "That's what's great about Awards Night. You just never know who will win what." Still, we spent a lot of the meeting trying to guess. And before I knew it, it was 6:00 and time to wrap things up. Another BSC meeting had come and gone.

CHAPTER 3

"I can't believe how heavy this stuff gets after five blocks," I said. "Are you okay, David Michael?" I looked down at my little brother. He was lugging a big duffel bag that clanked as it bumped along the sidewalk. It clanked because it was filled with softball bats. We were on our way to the first Krushers–Bashers practice game of the season. It was kind of a gray, overcast day, but the rain hadn't started yet. I was hoping it would wait a while.

"No problem," said David Michael, panting a little. "I can handle this stuff as long as I don't have to carry *that*!" He pointed at the duffel bag I was carrying. It was even bigger than his, and it was filled with all kinds of equipment —bases, softballs, mitts, and a catcher's mask. There were even a few miscellaneous objects in there, like a purple hairbow that belonged to Hannie Papadakis (I'd picked it up near home plate after our last

20

practice), a G.I. Joe action figure that I thought belonged to Buddy Barrett, and a pair of sneakers that said *Claire Pike* on them, in red Magic Marker. Honestly, the kids on my team would forget their *heads* if they weren't screwed on. I am always picking up after them.

"It's not that heavy," I said to David Michael. "Besides, I'm not exactly *carrying* it." I was kind of jerking it along the sidewalk. I stopped to rest for a second. It's a pretty long walk from our house to Stoneybrook Elementary, where we hold our practices. And it feels even longer when I have to bring all that stuff along. If Watson is home he usually drives me. He's a big help with all kinds of Krushers' stuff — sometimes I teasingly call him my "assistant manager." But that day he had an important meeting, so I was on my own. I sure was glad to have David Michael's help.

"So Jake is getting to be pretty good, huh?" David Michael asked as we started to walk again. I'd told him how Jake and I had practiced his pitching.

"He is," I said. "I'm definitely going to start using him more in games. I think he's ready."

"That's great," said David Michael. He sounded just a little envious. David Michael has been known as kind of a klutz, but he's been really trying hard lately to overcome that image. I think he dreams of being a really good athlete.

"*You're* getting really good, too," I said. "You were part of that great double play during our last practice." Kids — especially the kind of kids who are Krushers — need a lot of encouragement if they're going to improve. I've discovered that there's no such thing as too much praise, at least not when it comes to the kids on my team.

"Yeah," said David Michael. He sounded unconvinced.

"Come on, your timing was great," I said. "Not everybody could have done what you did. Hey! Look at that!" I pointed across the street, at a construction site where a few houses were being built. I thought it might be best to get David Michael's attention focused on something other than his softball skills, or lack of them.

"Wow!" he said. "Last week that was just an empty lot. I can't believe how fast those houses are going up." He walked a little slower for a few minutes as he watched a work crew climb around on the skeletonlike frame of one house. He'd forgotten about softball for the moment.

Have you ever noticed how boys — no matter what age they are — can stand and watch heavy machinery or trucks, or even just a bunch of guys with hammers, for *hours* at a time? They never seem to get tired of it. Me, I'm bored within thirty seconds. I pulled David Michael along. "We're going to be late," I said.

Mallory was the first person I saw when we walked onto the school playground. "Hey, Mal," I said as I dropped my duffel bag to the ground. "What are you doing here?"

"I'm sitting for Charlotte, and she and Vanessa had planned to be here to cheer for you," she said. "So we all came over."

"Hi, Kristy!" yelled Charlotte and Vanessa. They said it in unison, as if it were a cheer. I laughed.

"Hi, you two," I said. "I'm glad you could come." They were wearing their cheerleader outfits: denim skirts, sneakers, knee socks, and, of course, "Kristy's Krushers" T-shirts. Vanessa is one of Mallory's younger sisters. She isn't into sports at all, but she wanted to be part of our team somehow. That's why she's a cheerleader. She's made up some pretty good cheers, too. Vanessa's ambition is to be a poet, and she's good at rhymes. Charlotte Johanssen is a girl we sit for fairly often. I was shocked when she agreed to be a cheerleader, since she'd always been extremely shy. But she's coming out of her shell, and she seems to love jumping around and yelling along with the others.

23

I looked over at the ball field and saw that most of my players were already there. Mallory followed my gaze. "The other team isn't here yet," she said, sounding worried. "Does that mean the game is cancelled?"

"No," I said. "I told my kids to be here a half hour early. I wanted them to have a chance to warm up before the Bashers arrive." I looked up at the sky and frowned. "I just hope the rain holds off. I'd hate to have to reschedule this game. The Krushers are really up for it.

"Okay, gang," I yelled to the kids who were milling around on the field. "Let's get started!" They ran to me. As they gathered around I looked at their eager faces, and a feeling of pride washed over me. A lot of my players have come a long way since the team started. Jamie Newton, for example. He's only four years old, so it wasn't a surprise that he was kind of afraid of the ball when we began. And don't get me wrong, he still is. But he's a lot better about it. At least now he doesn't flinch every time it comes his way.

And Claire, Mallory's youngest sister. She's five. She used to throw the most horrendous tantrums whenever things didn't go her way, when she struck out, for example. But now she just stamps her foot and pouts for a second, and then she's over it.

"Hi, Kristy," yelled Jake Kuhn. He was standing near the back of the crowd, tossing a ball up in the air and catching it neatly on its way down. "Do you need me to pitch today?" He sounded hopeful.

"Probably not right away," I said, "since Nicky is here." Nicky Pike, one of Mallory's little brothers (this team would be a lot smaller without the Pike family!), is our regular pitcher, and he looked ready to go. "But you'll pitch soon, I promise." I bent over and started to pull equipment out of the bags, but then I realized something. Where were Laurel and Patsy? They usually arrive along with Jake. I stood up again. "Hey, Jake," I said. "Where are your sisters?"

"Don't you remember?" he asked. "They had to go to the dentist."

"Oh, right," I said. Mrs. Kuhn had told me that the day before. I'd totally forgotten. "Okay, ready for drills?" I asked, passing out gloves and bats and balls. "Everybody out in the field!"

I hit balls to the kids for about ten minutes, making sure that everybody had a chance to field at least one grounder and one fly ball. Then I pitched for batting practice. Everybody got five swings, although more often than not they'd end up pleading for: "One more, *please*, Kristy?" I was pitching to Buddy Barrett when

Mary Anne arrived with Matt and Haley Braddock.

"Sorry we're late," she called. "I'm sitting for these guys today, and it took us a while to get out of the house. Matt couldn't find his T-shirt, and Haley couldn't find her knee socks."

"I'm just glad you made it," I said. And I was. Matt's one of our best players, even though he's deaf. The rest of the team has learned how to communicate with him, using some basic sign language. And his sister Haley's arrival meant that our full cheerleading squad was on hand.

I finished up batting practice by pitching to Gabbie Perkins, who's two and a half. We use a wiffle ball when she's at bat, and the pitcher has to stand about five yards away from her. Bart has been very understanding about this, although some of the kids on his team used to tease us for having a baby on our team. They used to tease us about a *lot* of stuff, in fact. They even used to call Jake Kuhn "fatso"! I looked over at him and realized that he wasn't pudgy anymore. Anyway, the Bashers have learned some manners since we first started playing together, and now our games are usually very civilized.

Just as I threw the last pitch to Gabbie (she swung hard but missed it), Bart strode onto the field with his Bashers marching behind him. They like to make a grand entrance. "Hi, Bart," I said, smiling. Being around him still makes me feel a little nervous, but I'm getting used to it. At least I'm getting used to feeling as if I have butterflies in my stomach, rubber bands for legs, and a slight fever whenever I'm near him. "We're ready to play ball," I said. "How about you?"

"Ready," he answered. "As long as the weather cooperates." We both glanced at the sky. It was still heavy and gray, but no rain was falling yet.

"Let's start," I said. "At least we can play a few innings before the rain comes." The Krushers took the field, and the game began.

Within three innings, the score was ten to nothing. The Bashers, as usual, were winning by a mile. But you know what? It didn't matter. I could tell that my team felt good just being out there playing. They know that the Bashers are hard to beat; after all, most of Bart's kids are older than most of mine. The Krushers don't always expect to win. All I ask of them, and all they ask of themselves, is to play their best. Anyway, it was just a practice game.

So it didn't matter much when Claire wasted a big hit by getting so excited that she ran the bases backward. Or when Nicky let loose with a wild pitch that ended up in the third baseman's glove. Or when Matt got carried away and tried to steal when I had clearly signed him to "hold up."

We knew we'd do better next time.

When the game was over (I don't even want to tell you the final score), Bart offered to help me and David Michael carry the equipment home. He lives near me, so we often end up walking home together from games. "Sure," I said. "But let me just talk to Jake for a minute, first." I'd noticed that Jake looked a little down, so I made sure to tell him that he'd be pitching in a game really soon. He looked happier after that. Then I asked him who was walking him home.

"No one," he said. "Mom's with Laurel and Patsy. She said I could walk home by myself."

"You'd better *run* home," said Bart, who had overheard. He pointed to the sky, which was darker than ever. "It's going to pour any minute."

"Okay, 'bye!" said Jake, and he trotted off toward his house. We watched him go, then turned and headed in the opposite direction.

CHAPTER 4

Bart took the equipment bag that David Michael was lugging. "Here, let me carry that," he said. "We'd better walk home really fast, or else we're going to get soaked."

David Michael looked at him gratefully. So did I. Bart is such a thoughtful guy. You might think that I'd be insulted that he didn't offer to take *my* bag, but Bart knows me too well to offer that. He knows I'm not some sweet little thing who's afraid to use her muscles. I would have been insulted if he *had* offered to carry it.

We started out walking, and Bart set a pretty fast pace. I hurried to keep up with him, and David Michael trotted between us. "Good game today," I said to Bart. "Congratulations!"

"Thanks," he said. "I thought both teams did well. You were looking great at first base, David Michael," he added.

"Really?" said David Michael. His face lit up.

"Absolutely," answered Bart. "You must be getting some really good coaching somewhere," he added. He smiled at me over David Michael's head. It was a special, private kind of a smile.

"Uh, so, when should we schedule another game?" I asked quickly. My face suddenly felt hot, and I hoped Bart couldn't tell that I was blushing.

"Next week would be fine," said Bart. "Or whenever you're ready. We can talk about it."

I nodded, and switched my duffel bag to my other shoulder. I looked up at the sky. I couldn't believe that the rain hadn't started yet.

"Wow!" said Bart, coming to a dead stop in the middle of the sidewalk. "Awesome." He was looking at the construction site.

"I know," said David Michael. "Isn't that crane the coolest?"

"I wish I knew how to drive one of those front-end loaders," said Bart dreamily.

Front-end loaders? What were they? All those huge machines look alike to me. I rolled my eyes. "Hey, guys," I said, snapping my fingers in front of Bart's face. "We were on our way home, remember? And it's about to — "

30

Before I could finish my sentence (I was going to say "pour"), the rain started to come down in buckets. I was soaked within about two seconds.

"Oh, no!" yelled David Michael. "We aren't even halfway home yet!"

We started to run, dodging the puddles that had already appeared. I was dragging the equipment bag behind me, and it bumped along wildly.

Bart shook his wet hair out of his eyes. "Need a hand?" he called.

"What I *need* is an umbrella!" I yelled. "I'm drenched!"

Bart gave me a devilish grin. "Then you won't care if I do *this*!" he said, jumping into a puddle next to me so that it splashed all over my legs. I gave a yell, but you know what? I didn't care. I was already saturated, so a little more water didn't make any difference. I laughed.

"Bart Taylor," I said menacingly, "you are going to get it!" I chased after him and jumped into a huge puddle, sending the spray all over him.

"Why, you little . . ." he said, grinning. His face was wet all over, and he looked, all of a sudden, like a ten-year-old kid. He ran to me then and put his hand on my shoulder. His face came nearer to mine. Oh my lord! Was he going to —

Just then, David Michael kicked a big fountain of water all over *both* of us. Then he took off. We ran after him, laughing and shaking the water off as we headed toward home.

When we reached my house, I asked Bart in. "You might as well stay here until the rain lets up a little," I said. He agreed. We went into the kitchen, where it was nice and warm. Nannie was baking cookies, and they smelled delicious. "Chocolate chip?" I asked, hugging her.

"Kristy Thomas, what *are* you doing?" she said, laughing. "You are soaking wet, and you're getting me wet, too. Why don't you find some towels. By the time you dry off the cookies will be done. They're for my bowling league potluck supper, but you can have a few. And yes, they're chocolate chip."

I ran upstairs to the linen closet and grabbed an armful of towels. Then I brought them downstairs and passed them out to Bart and David Michael. We all sat around the kitchen table, rubbing ourselves dry and breathing in the smell of Nannie's cookies.

Nannie's great at baking, but she doesn't do it that often. She usually doesn't have time! She's not like a storybook grandmother, who spends her days baking and knitting. She goes bowling, and drives around in her cool pink car (we call it the Pink Clinker), and volunteers at different places like the library and the Foodshelf. Plus she spends a lot of time taking care of Emily Michelle. Who was, at the moment, asleep in her crib. Which was why Nannie had time to bake those cookies.

"Well, I hope you like them," she said, putting a plate down in the middle of the table. "I tried something a little different this time. More chips and fewer walnuts."

David Michael took one in each hand. Bart was a little more polite — he just took one. "Wow, these are great," he said. "I think I like them this way."

"Me, too," I agreed. "The chips are the best part." I got up and poured us each a glass of milk, and then the three of us sat and ate cookies until only crumbs were left on the plate. Nannie watched us, smiling.

"Well, I hate to eat and run," said Bart, "but it looks as if the rain is over, and I better get home." He stood up and handed me the towel. "Thanks," he said. "That was fun."

"It was," I agreed, knowing that he was talking about the whole afternoon, not just the cookie part. I walked him to the door. "See you," I called as he headed down the walk.

I heard the phone ring as I turned back into the house. "Kristy," called Nannie. "It's for you."

I ran to the kitchen and picked up the phone. "Hello?" I said.

"Kristy, it's Caroline Kuhn. I was just wondering — is Jake with you?"

"Jake?" I asked, taken by surprise. "No, he headed home after practice. He said it was okay with you if he walked by himself." Oh, no, I thought. Had Jake made that up? Should I have insisted on walking him home?

"Oh," Mrs. Kuhn replied. "He was right. I *did* say that. Anyway, Jake's not here, but I only just got home with the girls. Maybe he's been here and gone already. He might have gone to Buddy's house and forgotten to leave me a note. I'll try calling the Barretts'." She didn't sound too worried.

"Good idea," I said. "I hope you track him down soon." I hung up and turned to clean off the kitchen table. Then I helped Nannie start dinner, which was going to be chili and rice. I put the water on to boil and measured out the rice. Then I began to make a salad.

Just as I was finishing that job, the phone rang again. I put down the knife I was using to cut up carrots, and picked up the receiver. "Hello?" I said.

"Kristy, it's Caroline Kuhn again. There's still no sign of Jake. I've called every friend of his that I can think of, and nobody's seen him. Have you heard from him?"

"No, I haven't," I said. "Wow, I wonder where he is."

"I'm going to go looking for him in my car," she said. She was beginning to sound pretty worried. "The rain has stopped, but he must be soaked, wherever he is. He'll be glad to get a ride home."

"I'll make some calls," I said. "Maybe one of my friends has seen him."

"That would be great," said Mrs. Kuhn. "I'll check in with you in about a half hour."

I called Mary Anne and Dawn, Claudia, and Jessi. None of them had seen Jake Kuhn. Claud said she'd call Stacey for me, and Jessi offered to call Mal. "Maybe he's at the library or something," said Jessi. "Maybe he remembered some homework he had to do."

"Could be." I didn't really think that was likely. Still, I called the library to ask if he was there. No one had seen him. And I didn't hear back from Stacey or Mal, so I figured they hadn't seen him either.

The phone rang again right after I'd called Bart to let him know what had happened. It was Mrs. Kuhn again, and she didn't sound all that worried anymore. Now she sounded mad.

"I've figured it out," she said. "Harry must have taken him."

Harry? "Mr. Kuhn?" I asked, guessing.

"That's right," she said. "He wanted to take Jake to Europe, and I said no. So he just decided to come and *take* him. I can't believe it!"

I couldn't believe it either. "Are you sure?" I asked.

"It's the most likely explanation," she said. "Harry hates to take no for an answer. And Jake would have jumped right into the car with him. He was *so* disappointed when I wouldn't let him go on that trip."

I shuddered, imagining Jake jumping into a car. The idea was kind of creepy. Why do adults have to act so weird when they get divorced?

"As soon as they've had time to fly back to Texas, I'm going to call Harry and give him a piece of my mind," said Mrs. Kuhn. "Thanks for your help, Kristy."

I couldn't figure out what I'd done to help, but it was nice of her to thank me anyway. "You're welcome," I said. "Good luck!" I didn't know what else to say. I hung up and stood there looking at the phone. Suddenly I felt a pang of guilt. After all, I'd been the last one to see Jake. If he was really missing, maybe it was partly my fault. I thought again about Jake jumping into a car. If he *had* done that, I sure hoped it *was* Mr. Kuhn's car. What if Jake had jumped into a stranger's car? I shuddered. Wherever Jake was, I just hoped he was safe.

Wow! Things are even crazier than usual in the Pike household. For that matter, things are pretty crazy for sleepy old Stoneybrook, Connecticut. It seems as if everyone's looking for Jake Kuhn. I can't believe he's actually missing. Neither can Laurel and Patsy. I don't think they understand exactly what's going on, but they know something's up. And it's making them pretty anxious and upset. I wish I knew how to comfort them.

Mallory was feeling pretty anxious and upset herself that evening. After giving the situation more thought, Mrs. Kuhn had decided she couldn't ignore the possibility that Jake might be in serious trouble. She began her own search. She'd called Mrs. Pike to ask if she could watch Laurel and Patsy for a while. Mrs. Kuhn must have realized that her search would be more complicated with the girls along, and that her worrying would only upset them. She and Mrs. Pike are good friends, and Laurel and Patsy are friends with Margo and Claire, so it was natural for her to bring them to the Pikes' house.

So, while I was home making phone calls, Mal was helping her mom deal with a houseful of kids. All of her brothers and sisters were home, so when you added Patsy and Laurel, that made *nine* kids, plus Mal! Mal was trying to keep them busy while her mom figured out what to have for dinner.

"Adam!" Mallory said. "My dearest darling favorite triplet-with-a-name-beginning-with-A!"

(Adam is the *only* triplet with a name beginning with A. The other triplets' names are Byron and Jordan.)

"What do you want me to do?" Adam asked.

"Take your brothers and set the table for twelve. You set out the glasses, Jordan can set out the plates, Adam can do silverware, and Nicky can fold napkins. Have a race. See who gets his job done first."

"Right, sir!" said Adam, saluting. "Fall in, men!" he said to his brothers. "About face! Forward march!" He led the parade into the dining room. The triplets are ten, and Nicky's eight. They're old enough to be responsible about doing jobs around the house. They're also old enough to give Mal a hard time about bossing them around.

"Now," said Mallory, turning to the five girls who were left with her in the rec room. "Let's see. How about — " She thought fast. What would be a good activity to keep everyone entertained until dinner? "How about a Barbie fashion show?" she asked.

"Yea!" Claire squealed. She's five, and she *loves* to play with her Barbies. "I just got a new outfit for my Skipper. It's for going bowling!"

"I get to put Barbie's wedding dress on!" yelled Margo. She's seven, and lately she's been obsessed with weddings. Mal says she talks about them all the time. What kind of flowers the bride should carry, how long her train should be — all that stuff.

Mal noticed that Patsy and Laurel were hanging back. "I know you guys don't have your Barbies with you," she said. "But we've got a whole bunch of them here. You can take your pick." There are about a zillion Barbies in the Pike household. That's what happens when you have four girls growing up in one home. Laurel and Patsy squatted down by the toy chest and started to pull out various pieces of Barbie clothing.

Vanessa was standing in the doorway with her arms folded. "And what am *I* to do today?" she asked. "I'm too old for Barbie play."

Remember I told you that Vanessa wants to be a poet? Well, to keep in practice, she tries to speak in rhyme whenever possible. It drives Mal crazy.

Mal rolled her eyes. She knew that Vanessa did, occasionally, still play with Barbies — which meant that Vanessa's question had just been an excuse for a rhyme. But she didn't want to argue. "Why don't you be the judge of the fashion show?" she asked. "We can have prizes for Fanciest Outfit, Silliest Outfit, or whatever else you can think of." She rummaged around in the art supplies kept on a shelf. "Here, these stickers can be the prizes."

Vanessa looked satisfied with her new role, and the hour before dinner flew by without any more problems. Still, Mal was relieved when her mom called to say that dinner was ready. Mr. Pike was home from work by then, and he helped to make sure everyone's hands were washed and that everyone had a seat at the crowded table.

Mrs. Pike had made a huge pot of spaghetti, since she knows it's a food that most kids will eat.

Of course, there are always exceptions.

"I *hate* spaghetti!" said Patsy as soon as she saw her plate.

"Patsy!" said Laurel. "You're not supposed to say that when you're being company at somebody else's house." She looked over at Mrs. Pike. "She doesn't know," she said. "She's only five."

"You be quiet!" said Patsy, frowning at Laurel. "You're not the boss of me!"

Mallory realized that Patsy was probably missing her mom, and also feeling a little anxious about her routine being disrupted. "Mom, don't we have some hot dogs in the fridge?" she asked. Mrs. Pike nodded. "Do you like hot dogs?" she said, turning to Patsy.

"I *love* hot dogs!" said Patsy.

"So do I!" cried Adam.

"Me too!" cried Claire.

"Hot dogs, hot dogs, we want hot dogs!" yelled about five kids at once.

Mrs. Pike looked sadly at her huge pot of spaghetti. Then she looked at Mal and shrugged. "Go ahead," she said. "Boil up some hot dogs, if that's what everyone wants." Mrs. Pike doesn't waste time arguing with the kids over what they eat. If she did that with all eight kids, she wouldn't have time left to do anything else!

So Mal went into the kitchen and got the hot dogs out of the fridge. She was just putting a pan of water on to boil when the phone rang. "Hello?" said Mal, sticking the receiver under her chin as she checked the flame on the stove.

"Mal, it's Jessi. Kristy called an emergency club meeting. Can you come?" Jessi sounded tense.

"Now that my dad's home, I'm sure I can. It's about Jake, right?" asked Mal.

"Right," said Jessi. "Come over to Claud's as soon as you can, okay?"

By the time Mal got to the meeting, the rest of us were already there. All except Mary Anne, that is.

"She's going nuts trying to hem this dumb skirt she made," explained Dawn. "It's supposed to be done tomorrow, and she just can't get the hang of that kind of stitch you're supposed to use — you know, the one where the sewing doesn't show?"

"The slip stitch," said Stacey. "I know how to do that. It *is* kind of hard, though."

"Poor Mary Anne," said Logan, shaking his

42

head. He and Shannon, our associate members, were both there for the emergency meeting, since I had decided that the more brains we had in the room, the better. "She told me when I called that she'd already ripped it out three times. She sounded like she was about to lose her temper."

"Mary Anne?" I said. "Lose her temper? I don't believe it." Mary Anne is such a mouse most of the time. I realized that the home-ec problem must really be worrying her.

"Well, anyway," I went on. "We have much more important things to talk about. Is everyone up-to-date on the situation with Jake Kuhn?"

My friends nodded.

"You know," said Mal. "I have to say that I just don't think Mrs. Kuhn is right about her husband taking Jake away. I mean, today at the game? When his team was up at bat? We were talking, and he couldn't stop telling me about his Turtle birthday party. He is *so* excited about it. I just don't think he'd leave Stoneybrook right before that party."

I nodded. "I was thinking the same thing," I said. "Plus, I told him that he'll be pitching for the Krushers soon. I know he wouldn't want to miss *that*, either."

Just then the phone rang. I nearly jumped out of my skin. Could it be Mrs. Kuhn, calling to say that Jake was home safe?

"It's Mary Anne," said Claud, who had grabbed the phone. "She's still working on that hem, but she wanted to check in."

I let out a breath. "Tell her thanks — and that there's no news yet," I said. Claud repeated the message.

"You know what else?" said Dawn. "My mom says she's known Harry Kuhn since he was a little kid, and that he was always really decent. I don't think she believes he'd steal his own kid, and I don't either."

"My parents like Mr. Kuhn, too," said Claudia. "Mom says he volunteers every single year for the library's book sale." (Mrs. Kishi is head librarian at the Stoneybrook library.)

I didn't think that volunteering at the library proved Mr. Kuhn was innocent, but I had to agree with the others. He probably hadn't taken Jake. But what if he was really, really upset about missing his son's birthday? Maybe he was desperate. Still, I just didn't think Jake would have gone with his dad, even if Mr. Kuhn had tried to kidnap him. What a mess. The emergency meeting wasn't getting us anywhere, but it was good to be together, talking about Jake. The situation was pretty scary. A *kid* was *missing*.

I heard the doorbell ring, and Claud's phone rang at exactly the same time. It was Mary Anne. On the phone, that is. Stacey gave her an update while the rest of us helped ourselves to the Doritos Claud was passing around. I had just put a handful of them into my mouth when I heard a knock on the door.

"Come in," said Claud. The door opened, and I saw Claud's sister Janine standing there with a strange look on her face.

Behind her were two policemen, one tall, and one short and wide. "We're looking for Kristy Thomas," the tall one said, in a deep voice.

I almost choked on my Doritos. "That's me!" I answered, after I'd coughed until tears were coming out of my eyes.

"Your mother said you'd be here. We understand you were the last person to see the missing boy today. His mother seems fairly sure about what happened to him, but while we're trying to locate Mr. Kuhn, we're also doing a neighborhood check. We'd like to ask you some questions."

I told the cops everything I knew, and gave them my opinion on the case, too — even though they didn't ask for it.

By the time we finished up our meeting and Mal went back home that night, she felt pretty confused and tired. And she found two confused and tired girls waiting for her there. Patsy and Laurel. It had been a long day for them, too.

CHAPTER 6

After the emergency meeting, Shannon and I went outside to wait for Charlie to pick us up. Shannon lives across the street from me, which is how we met in the first place. She goes to a private school, not to SMS, so I'd never even seen her until I moved. It's nice to have a friend in my neighborhood, since I live so far from my old friends now.

We sat down to wait on the Kishis' front steps. "I just can't believe it," I said, shaking my head. "One minute Jake is there, and the next . . ."

"I know," said Shannon. "How could a kid just *disappear*?"

"You hear about these things happening," I said. "You see those kids' pictures on milk cartons. But you never think about it happening to a kid you *know*."

"Maybe he's not really missing, though," said Shannon. "I bet he'll turn up soon. Those kids on the milk cartons have been missing for months, or even years."

Months! Years! I couldn't *begin* to imagine how I would feel if Jake were gone that long. Not to mention how Mrs. Kuhn would feel. Just then I heard a car horn. "There's Charlie!" I said, standing up. But then I got a closer look at the car. It was our green station wagon, not Charlie's Junk Bucket. And my mom was driving.

Shannon and I walked to the car and got in. "Hi, Mrs. Brewer," said Shannon.

"Hi, Mom," I said. "How come you're picking us up instead of Charlie?"

"I wanted to stop in and see Caroline Kuhn," she said. My mom and Mrs. Kuhn have been friends for a while, ever since they started to take this aerobics class together. "I thought you'd want to come with me," she continued.

"Sure," I said. "I wonder if there's any news."

"Don't get your hopes up," my mom said. "When I called Caroline to let her know I was coming, she still hadn't heard anything."

"Is she upset?" I asked.

"Very," said my mom. "And very angry at Harry. She's still pretty sure he took Jake."

"What do you think?" I asked. "Do you think he did it?"

"Oh, hon, I don't know," said my mom. "I would never have thought Harry was capable of doing something like that, but divorce *does* make people do strange things."

I was quiet for a moment. I started to think about seeing Mrs. Kuhn. I wondered if she blamed me at all for Jake's disappearance. After all, I had been the last person to see her son. The last person. I couldn't stop picturing him in my head. I could see him as plain as day, waving and smiling as he started toward home. How could I have let him go off alone, even if it *was* okay with his mom? Normally I'm so responsible it's sickening.

Maybe I'd been distracted by the fact that Bart was waiting to walk me home. Maybe I'd just been thinking about *myself*. Maybe everything was my fault. I closed my eyes tight and let out a groan.

"What's the matter, sweetie?" asked my mom. "Does you stomach hurt? I *told* you not to rush through your supper."

"I'm fine," I said. But I *was* feeling kind of sick to my stomach. The thought of facing Mrs. Kuhn was suddenly beginning to make me wish that our station wagon was heading in any direction *except* toward the Kuhns' house. I felt horrible.

"Um, Mrs. Brewer?" asked Shannon as my mom parked the car in front of the Kuhns'. "I think I'll just wait in the car. I don't really know the Kuhns, and it looks as if they've got enough company already." She gestured at the cars that were parked on the street. I counted at least six, plus two police cars.

"That sounds fine, Shannon," said my mom. "We won't be long."

"See you," I said to Shannon, as I got out of the car. My throat felt like it had closed up. How was I going to talk to Mrs. Kuhn? Mom and I walked toward the house.

The place was lit up from top to bottom, and the front door was open wide. Light streamed out onto the front lawn. I heard lots of people talking at once. A police radio squawked and a static-y voice boomed out, but I couldn't tell what the voice was saying. I felt as if I was walking in slow motion, which was fine with me. The slower the better. Maybe if I walked slowly enough, Jake would be home by the time I reached the front door.

"Kristy, please stop dawdling," said my mother impatiently. Then she took a closer look at my face. "Is something wrong?" she asked, more gently.

"I'm fine," I said. "I *told* you, I'm fine." My mother tightened her lips and shook her head at me. I couldn't believe I'd just snapped at her. I hardly ever do that. But I was feeling so, so nervous about seeing Mrs. Kuhn. "I'm sorry," I said quickly. "It's just that — "

"Caroline!" said my mother, looking up toward the house. "Any news?"

Mrs. Kuhn shook her head sadly. She was standing in the doorway, framed by light. I saw a policeman in the hall behind her, talking into his radio. "I'm glad you came by, though. Everybody's being so supportive — it's really wonderful. It's times like these when you realize what good friends you have."

"I just wish there was something I could do," said my mom.

"There's nothing *anyone* can do," replied Mrs. Kuhn. "Unless you know where Harry is. We can't locate him, and until we find him there's nothing we can do but wait. Why don't you come in?"

I had been kind of standing in the shadows behind my mom, but I figured I had to show myself at some point. Now was as good a time as any. I stepped out so that Mrs. Kuhn could see me. I cleared my throat. "Um — " I began.

"Kristy!" said Mrs. Kuhn. "I didn't see you there. Come on in and have some cake. Everybody's been bringing food over, for some reason. I guess they just want to *do* something. Everybody's been so helpful with the girls, too — they're staying at the McGills' tonight."

At the McGills'? I thought they were at Mal's.

My mom and I walked into the house, and there I was, standing right next to Mrs. Kuhn. I took a deep breath. "Mrs. Kuhn," I said, a little too loudly. I toned it down a bit. "Mrs. Kuhn, I just want to say that I'm really, really sorry. I feel like this is my fault — "

"Stop right there," said Mrs. Kuhn. "Please, don't apologize. There is no way this is your fault. I know that you are an incredibly responsible baby-sitter, and that you would never let a child go off alone unless you knew it was all right. And I had given Jake permission to walk home alone."

"But — " I said.

Mrs. Kuhn went on, ignoring my interruption. "Please, just don't feel guilty," she said. "This is bad enough without second-guessing ourselves about what we *could* have done or *should* have done."

I nodded. I knew she was right. I knew it wasn't my fault, and I'd known it in my heart all along. But somehow, apologizing had made me feel much better. "We had an emergency meeting of our club tonight," I told Mrs. Kuhn. "We want to help find Jake."

"That's nice," she said vaguely. I got the feeling she didn't think that a bunch of middle school girls could do much to help. "Why don't you help yourself to some cake?" she suggested again, pointing toward the dining room table. Then she turned to my mother. "I have tried *everything* I can think of to find Harry," she said, sounding frazzled.

"Why don't you tell me what you've tried so far, and maybe together we can think of something else," said my mom. I hung around for a minute, hoping to hear what Mrs. Kuhn had done. But my mom turned and saw me. "Go on, Kristy," she said. Obviously, she didn't think there was any reason for me to be listening.

I walked over to the food table, feeling like a little kid who's been told to stand in the corner. I helped myself to a piece of carrot cake, even though I wasn't hungry at all. As I stood there eating it, I could hear scraps of the conversation between Mrs. Kuhn and my mom.

" — just can't imagine where Harry could have taken him," Mrs. Kuhn was saying.

"Oh, Caroline," said my mom. "You must be so worried. Have you tried — "

My mom's question was drowned out by a blast of static from the policeman's radio. How annoying. If I was going to help find Jake, I needed all the information I could get.

Before I'd even finished my carrot cake, my mom came to find me. "Let's go," she said. "I think Caroline is feeling a little overwhelmed. I'll check in with her in the morning."

We drove Shannon home and then pulled in to our own driveway. I ran indoors, headed straight for the phone, and dialed Bart's number. I don't call him very often — I still feel kind of shy about it — but that night I really needed to talk to him. After all, he'd been with me when I said good-bye to Jake, and I knew he'd understand how I was feeling. We talked for a long time.

After I hung up, I felt exhausted. I climbed into bed without even brushing my teeth. I turned out the lamp and lay in the dark. It was pitch-black outside by then. Where could Jake be? I had been sure he'd be home safe in his bed by this time. I thought of him out there in the night. Was he afraid? Was he feeling lonely? Was he homesick?

Just as I was about to drift off to sleep, I realized that I hadn't even *looked* at my homework that night. But you know what? I didn't care. All I cared about was finding Jake.

CHAPTER 7

Thursday

Wow! This has been some day. I can't believe that such a boring, normal Thursday (I had a math test at school, I wrote an essay for English, when I got home, I had pork chops for dinner) turned into such a dramatic, scary day for all of us. And I just hate the thought that no matter how scared the rest of us are, Jake, wherever he is, might be even more scared. At least Patsy and Laurel are hanging in there. Maybe it's lucky that they're too young to understand. And I think they're better off staying with friends. Being at home with all those policemen hanging around would probably be really, really frightening for them.

That evening when Stacey had gotten home from our meeting, she found out that Mrs. Kuhn had brought Patsy and Laurel over to spend the night. She'd told Stacey's mom that she hated to impose on the Pikes, since they didn't have much room for two extra kids.

Stacey's mom was glad to help out. I think she feels a special kind of closeness with Mrs. Kuhn, since she's been through a divorce recently, too.

Mrs. Kuhn had asked Stacey's mom not to tell the girls too much more about what was going on. She thought it would be traumatic for the girls to hear anyone talking about their father as if he were a kidnapper. That made sense to Stacey.

Stacey and her mom fixed up the guest room for the girls. Patsy and Laurel didn't seem to notice how upset their mom had been acting. They were too excited about "sleeping over" at Stacey's.

"Can we watch a movie?" asked Patsy.

"Can we stay up late?" asked Laurel. "Mommy lets us stay up late sometimes on special nights."

"Wellll," said Stacey. "I think it's a *little* too late to start a movie. Besides, I don't think my mom and I own any movies you two would like . . ."

"You don't even have *The Little Mermaid*?" asked Patsy, her eyes round. "I thought *everybody* had that."

"Sorry!" said Stacey. "But you know what we *do* have? A really great popcorn popper. And I think we should have a popcorn picnic. How about that?"

"What's a popcorn picnic?" asked Laurel.

"Well, it's something my mom and I do sometimes," answered Stacey. "We make a huge batch of popcorn, and then we divide it up and put different flavorings on it. We put butter on some, and grated cheese on some, and my mom even likes to put *cinnamon* on some and eat it with milk, like cereal! Then we take all the popcorn into the living room, spread out a blanket, and have a feast. Sometimes we do taste tests, to see whose recipe is the best."

"Yea!" said Patsy. "Popcorn picnics sound like fun."

Stacey was relieved that her idea had gone over so well. She herded the girls into the kitchen, started them singing "Bingo" (she knows that song takes a long time to finish), and set up the popcorn popper. She rustled around in the fridge and in the spice cabinet, and lined up some possible flavorings on the kitchen table.

By the time the popcorn was done, the girls

were on the last verse of their song. ". . . and Bingo was his name-o!" finished Laurel and Patsy just as Stacey was dividing the steaming popcorn into several small bowls.

"Okay, let's see," said Stacey. "I like to put parmesan cheese on mine." She reached for the shaker and gave her bowl a generous dose.

"How about this stuff?" asked Laurel, grabbing a spice bottle and shaking it over *her* bowl. "Wow, that smells strong!" she said.

"I hope you like garlic!" Stacey said, laughing. "You just dumped a whole lot of it onto your popcorn."

Laurel reached in and grabbed a handful. She put a kernel of popcorn into her mouth, chewed tentatively, and then gave Stacey a big smile. "I like it," she said. "It's good. It tastes kind of like pizza."

Meanwhile, Patsy had gotten busy with a few jars and bottles. "Look what I made," she said proudly, tilting her bowl so that Stacey could see.

"Oh gro — I mean, mmm, that looks good!" said Stacey. "What's that brown stuff?"

"I'm not sure," said Patsy. "It was in this bottle." She held up an empty container.

"Maple syrup?" asked Stacey. "Ew — I mean, that might be good. You never know. But I think you'll need some wet napkins with that, because it's going to be sticky." She went to the sink and moistened some napkins. "How about if we take our picnic into the living room," she said. "We can spread out this tablecloth and pretend we're outside." She picked up the tablecloth and her bowl of popcorn and led the girls, who carried *their* bowls, into the living room. They settled down, and Stacey began to think that her "picnic" idea was a success. Then she noticed that Patsy was sniffling as she ate.

"What's the matter, Patsy?" she asked.

"I miss Mommy," said Patsy. "And Jake. And Daddy. When will we get to be with them again?" She rubbed her eyes with her sticky fists.

"Soon, I hope," said Stacey. "You'll see your mommy first thing in the morning. I'll bring you home on my way to school."

"And maybe the policemen will have found Jake by then, too," said Laurel, looking hopeful.

"Maybe they will have," said Stacey.

"They better find him before his birthday," said Patsy. "He'll be sad if he misses his Turtle party. Especially since Daddy will probably come to it."

"Your father is coming to the party?" Stacey asked Laurel, over Patsy's head.

"No way," said Laurel. "He said he can't. I think Patsy just *wishes* he would."

"No, he *is* coming," said Patsy. "I saw his car, so I know he's here." She looked excited. Then she thought of something, and her face fell. "Except I don't know why he didn't come to see *me*. I miss Daddy, don't you?" She faced Laurel.

"Yeah," said Laurel. "But he lives very far away now, and he can't come visit all the time." Looking back at Stacey, she whispered, "She only *thinks* she saw Daddy's car. She's too little to know."

Stacey nodded. But she wondered. Patsy seemed so sure about seeing her father's car. Had anyone told Mrs. Kuhn — or the police — about that? What if Mr. Kuhn really *was* in the area? What if he had Jake and what if he was just waiting for the chance to take Patsy and Laurel, too? Stacey shivered.

"Time to finish up, you guys," she said. "Then you can brush your teeth and hop into bed. If you get into your pajamas right away, I'll read you a story."

The girls got ready for bed in record time, and they fell asleep before Stacey had even finished the first chapter of *The Indian in the Cupboard*. She turned out the light in the guest room and tiptoed downstairs to talk to her mom. She told her what Patsy had said. "Don't you think we should tell Mrs. Kuhn?" she asked.

"Absolutely," said her mother. "Go ahead and call her right now. The police are probably still over there, and they should hear about it, too."

When Stacey told Mrs. Kuhn about Patsy seeing — or *thinking* she saw — her dad's car, Mrs. Kuhn wasn't too surprised. And, like Laurel, she didn't put much stock in Patsy's sighting. "Patsy misses her father very much," she said. "It seems natural that she would think she'd seen his car. Also, I can't believe he'd drive it all the way from Dallas. Still, it's something we should look into. I'll make sure the police hear about it." Mrs. Kuhn thanked Stacey again for taking care of the girls. "I'll see you first thing in the morning," she said as she hung up.

Stacey spent the rest of the evening thinking hard about what might have happened to Jake. She told me later that she had a hard time falling asleep with the mystery left unsolved. I don't think any of us slept very well that night.

CHAPTER 8

I woke up and lay in bed for a moment, stretching and yawning. I could see that it was sunny and bright outside, which was a relief after all that rain. But as soon as I thought of the rain, I also thought of everything else that had happened the day before, and right away my stomach started to hurt.

Jake was missing.

The full weight of that fact hit me so hard that I almost felt like pulling the covers back over my head and hiding in bed all day. But the feeling only lasted a second. Then I began to have another, stronger feeling. I had to *do* something. I had to figure out a way to find Jake. It was time to take action.

I got dressed in a hurry and ran downstairs. "Any word from Mrs. Kuhn?" I asked my mother.

"She hasn't called this morning," said my mother. "And I'm afraid that in this case, no

61

news is not good news. She promised to call me right away if Jake was found." She sighed and shook her head sadly. "Poor Caroline," she said. "I can't imagine what she must be going through."

I sat down to eat breakfast, deep in thought. What could I do to find Jake? I didn't have the resources the police did: walkie-talkies, squad cars, computers. I thought some more as I ate my cereal and toast. I was concentrating so hard that I didn't even notice when David Michael joined me at the table. At least, I didn't notice him there until my mother pointed out that I hadn't saved him any toast.

"Kristy," she said. "What about your brother?"

My brother! That was it. Suddenly an idea came to me. It was exactly like in the cartoons, when a light bulb goes on over someone's head. I might not have the resources that the police had, but I had my brother and my friends' brothers and sisters and *their* friends! If we got enough kids together to search for Jake, maybe we could find him.

I knew that the police were already searching, and I knew that Mrs. Kuhn was almost sure that *Mr.* Kuhn had taken Jake. But something inside me just didn't believe that. Maybe Jake had gotten lost, or hurt — or both — on his way home from our Krushers' game. And maybe we could find him.

I think I was still feeling just a tiny bit guilty about Jake being missing. No matter how many times I told myself that it wasn't my fault, I couldn't help thinking that I'd been the last one to see him. I felt responsible.

But when I thought about organizing a search party, I felt much better. I'm the kind of person who needs to be *doing* things. I can't just sit around and worry. So while I finished my breakfast, I started to make a list of things to do. I used the back of a social studies handout, which was the only piece of paper I could find. Here's how my list started:

1) Emergency BSC meeting before homeroom — fill in other members on plan.

2) Talk to principal about setting up signup table during lunch.

3) Contact parents — get permission for kids to join search party.

4) Possible searchers — Matt and Haley Braddock, Adam, Jordan, and —

"Kristy!" said my mom, interrupting my list-making. "I've been trying to get your attention. You're about to miss your bus!"

"Thanks, Mom," I said, folding up the list and sticking it in my back pocket. I'd been concentrating so hard that I hadn't even heard her call my name the first couple of times.

As soon as the bus let me off in front of school, I started to round up the other BSC members. "I'm calling a quick emergency meeting," I told Mary Anne, who was the first person I found. "Help me get everyone together, okay?" We took off in opposite directions, and within minutes we'd gathered everyone except Jessi. She had gone into the building early.

"Jessi's lock isn't working right lately," Mal explained. "What's up? Did the police find Jake?"

I shook my head. "Unfortunately, they didn't. But listen, I have an idea. I think we should organize a big search party — all of us, plus the kids we sit for, plus any kids from our classes who want to help out. If we get a lot of people, we can really cover the neighborhood."

"That sounds great," said Stacey. "How do we let everyone know?" I told her about my idea for setting up a sign-up table at lunchtime, and she nodded. "Perfect. And we can divide up your list of kids so we'll each have to make only a few phone calls after school."

"I have study hall third period," said Claud. "I'll make a sign for the sign-up table then."

"I have to study for a stupid recipe test during *my* study hall," said Mary Anne. "But I can help organize the kids after school."

"I'll fill Jessi in on what's going on," said Mallory. "I don't think she has a dance class this afternoon. I'm sure she'll want to help."

"I think Jeff left his walkie-talkies in his room the last time he visited," said Dawn. "I'll bring them this afternoon. They might be useful."

We agreed that the search party would meet at the Stoneybrook Elementary playground right after school. I could tell that everyone was as happy as I was to be *doing* something.

As soon as I walked into homeroom, I asked my teacher for a pass to the principal's office. He gave it to me right away, when I'd explained why I needed it. And when I got to Mr. Taylor's office, she was great, too. Not only did she give me permission to set up a sign-up desk, she offered to let me make an announcement over the P.A. system during second period.

I spent the rest of homeroom feeling a little nervous about making the announcement, and also about the wheels I'd set in motion. All of a sudden the idea I'd had less than two hours ago at breakfast had sprung into life —and it was going to involve a *lot* of kids.

"What should I say?" I asked Mary Anne

while we were running from homeroom to our first class. "Do you think I'm going to sound all static-y? I hate that!"

"Just tell everyone what's going on," she said, "and tell them about your idea. Don't worry about sounding perfect." She smiled. "And yes, of course you're going to sound static-y. Why shouldn't you? Everyone else does. You'd just better hope in the middle of your speech that you don't get one of those noises that sounds like a jet landing."

"Mary *Anne*!" I wailed. "How could you say that? Oh, I hope that doesn't happen."

"It won't," she said. "I'm sorry I mentioned it. I know you're nervous. I'm not thinking straight right now. I'm trying to remember whether Jell-O is supposed to chill overnight or just for three hours. And when am I supposed to add the fruit?" She shook her head. "I'm sorry," she said again. "I know this home-ec stuff is nothing compared to Jake being lost. But if I don't pass this course . . ."

"I know, I know," I said. "It's all right. I'm sure my announcement will go okay. I'll just cross my fingers and hope I don't get that jet-engine sound." We said good-bye, and I headed for my first class, shaking my head. Mary Anne is usually so sensitive! Normally she'd never say anything that might upset me.

I couldn't believe how seriously she was taking her home-ec class.

Of course, the announcement went fine. Dawn told me later that she could hear every word, even though the static nearly drowned me out when I was explaining how the search parties would be organized.

At lunchtime, my friends and I took turns staffing the sign-up table. Claudia had made a great-looking sign. MISING SINSE LAST NIHGT!! it said, in giant purple letters. (Claud's not the world's greatest speller, but who cares? Her signs are always beautiful.) She'd drawn a sketch of Jake, and underneath it she'd written, *Help Us Finde Him!*

Lots of kids signed up. We told them to bring friends, too — and to tell their brothers and sisters. "We'll meet right after school," I said, over and over again. "At the playground."

The rest of the day crawled by. I could hardly sit still in math class, and social studies seemed more boring than ever. I couldn't wait to be outside, looking for Jake.

When school finally ended, Claudia and I practically *ran* over to her house. We went to her room and got busy on the phone. First I called Mrs. Kuhn to check in and let her know what we were planning. She had no news for me, and was beginning to sound kind of weepy. But I could tell she was holding herself together for Patsy and Laurel's sake. They'd spent the day with her, and she said she'd been trying to keep them busy with one activity after another.

"Maybe I shouldn't have kept them home from school," she said. "But I wanted them near me today." Before we hung up, we arranged for the girls to spend the night at my house that night. "If Jake isn't found by then, I know I'll be up all night again," she said. "And the police will be here, too. I think the girls need to get a good night's sleep."

Then Claud and I took turns calling a whole bunch of the parents we sit for, checking to make sure it was all right for their kids to join the search. And then, since it was almost time to meet everyone, we ran over to the elementary school.

I couldn't believe my eyes when I saw how many kids were at the playground. I hadn't been prepared for such a crowd. But Claudia and Mary Anne helped me divide the kids into teams, with at least one BSC member or older kid on each team. Then we figured out which part of the neighborhood each team should cover. It didn't take long. In a few minutes, teams set off in different directions and the playground was nearly empty again.

I was on a team with Stacey, David Michael, Matt and Haley Braddock, and Charlotte Johanssen. We started walking, following the route Jake would have taken home from the playground. We called for Jake every few steps.

"How were Laurel and Patsy this morning?" I asked Stacey.

"Hanging in there," she said. "I think they're scared, though. And Patsy keeps insisting she saw her dad last week. Isn't that weird?"

"Wow," I said. "She said the same thing to me before Jake even disappeared. I wonder if we should tell the police about that."

"I already did," said Stacey. "Or, anyway, I told Mrs. Kuhn. She was going to tell the police. But she didn't seem to think it meant much. She thinks Patsy's making it up because she misses her dad."

"She's probably right," I said. And then we dropped the subject and concentrated on looking for Jake.

CHAPTER
9

"JA-AKE!" I called.

"Hey, *Jake!*" yelled David Michael.

"Where *are* you, Jake?" shouted Stacey.

We walked along, stopping to call in different directions. Everyone was yelling for Jake — everyone, that is, but Matt Braddock. He couldn't call because he can't really speak; he's deaf, as I mentioned before. But I could see that he was *looking* as hard as he could. He peered into every backyard, searched the shadows beneath every bush, and checked out every garage we passed. He saw me watching him and he grinned at me. He signed a long sentence, and his sister Haley translated for me.

"He says that since he can't use his ears or his voice to help find Jake, he's trying his best to use his eyes and his brain."

"You're doing a great job," I replied, and when Haley translated for him, he looked at

70

me, shrugged, and signed again.

"Not good *enough* until we find Jake," Haley interpreted. I sighed and nodded.

We kept on walking and looking and calling, but I was beginning to feel that the search-party idea had been ridiculous. After all, Jake could be anywhere. Anywhere in Stoneybrook or even anywhere in the world! How could a bunch of kids and their baby-sitters hope to locate one little boy who could be *anywhere*?

"Don't worry, Kristy," said Stacey. She'd been walking beside me, and she must have seen my frown. "I *know* Jake will turn up soon."

"Yeah," said Charlotte, who was, as usual, sticking close to Stacey. Those two have a really special relationship — it's not just that Stacey is Charlotte's favorite sitter, or that Charlotte is Stacey's favorite kid — it's almost like they're sisters. "I know you'd find *me* if I were lost," she went on, looking up at Stacey. "Wouldn't you?"

"Of course," said Stacey, who knows that Charlotte sometimes needs a lot of reassurance. "I'd find you in a minute. I mean, in a nanosecond."

"A *what*?" I asked. Charlotte looked confused, too.

"A nanosecond," said Stacey. "It's a really, really small amount of time. A billionth of a second. We learned about it in math class the other day." She was smiling happily. Stacey just *loves* math. I don't hate it, but I can't relate to *loving* it.

"A nanosecond," I said. "Well, you learn something new every day."

"Very profound, Kristy," said Stacey, giggling. Then she slapped her hand over her mouth. "What am I doing?" she said. "How can I be laughing when Jake is missing?"

"It's okay," I said. "I mean, I know it's terrible that he's missing, but it doesn't mean the whole world has to come to a stop. We have to keep on doing our normal stuff — talking, and laughing, and going to school."

"Now you're *really* getting profound," said Stacey. "But you're right. I just wish we could do our normal stuff *and* find Jake."

Charlotte had been looking back and forth from me to Stacey as we talked. "*I* want to be profound," she said suddenly. "What *is* profound, anyway?"

Stacey and I cracked up, and then stopped laughing when we saw that Charlotte looked hurt. "We're not laughing at you, Char," said Stacey. "I just think you might want to wait a few years before you get profound. It's not important for eight-year-old kids to have really deep, heavy thoughts all the time."

"That's what it means?" asked Charlotte. "I'll wait."

Stacey and I were laughing again, when I felt a tap on my shoulder. It was Matt Braddock, and as soon as I looked at him, he started to sign really fast. I tried to follow what he was saying (I know a *little* sign language) but there was no way I could keep up. Matt looked awfully excited. I glanced over at Haley. "What's he saying?" I asked.

"He says he just remembered something," she replied. "He says there's this shortcut that Jake sometimes takes when he's walking home from school. Jake showed it to him one day after a Krushers' practice."

Matt doesn't go to Stoneybrook Elementary, so he wouldn't normally walk home with Jake. He goes to a special school for the deaf, in Stamford.

"Matt says he thinks there's a big drainage ditch — you know, with a pipe in it? — along the way," Haley went on. "He started to wonder if maybe Jake — "

"If Jake could be stuck in the pipe?" I asked, excited. "Oh, my lord! He could have crawled in there to get out of the rain, and then fallen asleep and not found out that he was stuck until he woke up!"

Haley told Matt what I'd said. He nodded

emphatically, and signed some more. "Or maybe the pipe leads into a sewer or something, and Jake is wandering around underground!" Haley looked terrified as she translated.

I kind of doubted that Jake was lost in a network of underground tunnels (that sounded a little farfetched), but if there was even a *chance* Jake was stuck in the pipe, I wanted to check it out as soon as I could. "Let's go!" I said. "Haley, ask Matt to lead us there."

We took off at a trot, following Matt. He led us through someone's backyard, over a small fence, and behind another house. We emerged on a quiet street and ran down it until we came to a vacant lot with a sign in front of it, advertising a new house that was about to be built.

"Where's the ditch?" I asked Matt. Haley didn't even have to translate. Matt understood what I was asking, and he pointed toward the back of the lot. We ran to a pipe, lying on its side in the mud. I could only see one opening, and it was just the right size for a boy to crawl into.

"Look!" said Charlotte, pointing at the ground near the ditch.

David Michael squatted down next to her. "Footprints!" he said.

"And they're not grown-up footprints, either!" said Haley, who had run over to look at them. "Maybe they're Jake's!"

My heart was beating fast. I looked at the small footprints — it appeared that someone who had been wearing sneakers had been walking around near the pipe — and then I bent down and peered into the pipe's opening. I half expected to see Jake peering back at me.

"*Jake!*" I yelled into the pipe.

" — *ake . . . ake . . . ake*," came the echo. And, just as I heard the echo, I saw daylight at the other end of the pipe, way off. That's when I knew that the pipe was empty. I stood up and looked down the length of the pipe from above. I saw it snake through the ditch until it was hidden in some undergrowth. But it wasn't that long. And it didn't go underground. And no little boy was hiding in it.

I shook my head. "He isn't in there," I said.

"But maybe he *was* in there for a while," said David Michael.

"Right," said Charlotte. "And then maybe he got out and went somewhere else! Let's follow these footprints."

I looked at Stacey and shrugged. "We might as well," I said. I had decided the footprints were too small to be Jake's, but we had nothing to lose by trying. I gave Matt a hug around the shoulders as we left the vacant lot. "It was a good idea," I said. Once again, he didn't need a translator to know what I had said. He signed back, and I didn't need one either.

"Not good enough," he was saying.

We followed the footprints until they disappeared when the person who made them stepped onto the sidewalk in front of the vacant lot. Then we continued along Jake's shortcut until we came out on the Kuhns' street. And there was Mary Anne, leading another group of searchers: the Pike triplets, Becca Ramsey, and a girl I didn't recognize.

"Any luck?" I asked, even though I knew what the answer would be.

"None," she said. "We've been calling and calling, but we haven't seen a sign of Jake anywhere. I'm *so* worried about him!"

Mary Anne looked as if she were about to cry.

"And now I have to quit and go home," she said. "I *have* to figure out what went wrong with that recipe today. Mrs. Ploof is giving me only one more chance to get it right. If I mess up again, that could be it."

"Go ahead," I said. "Stacey and I will make sure the kids get home safely. There's only another hour of daylight, anyway."

After Mary Anne left, Stacey and I decided to keep the kids busy searching the immediate neighborhood until it started to get dark. As we walked past the Kuhns' house, I noticed two police cars parked in front of it. I thought about how Mrs. Kuhn must be feeling as she watched another day come to an end with Jake still missing. I had had such high hopes of finding him, too. It was *so* frustrating to look and look and still not have anything to report.

Finally, when the streetlights started to come on, Stacey and I realized it was time to quit for the day. We walked the kids to their homes, and then I went to Stacey's to call my house and ask for a ride. Charlie picked me up half an hour later.

Patsy and Laurel were eating dinner with my family when I got home.

"We decided not to wait for you," said my mom. "But there's a plate of food for you in the oven."

"I'm not really hungry," I said. Mom looked as if she wanted to ask how the search had gone, but when she saw my face I guess she decided against it. I didn't want to say anything in front of Patsy and Laurel, so I waited until later to talk with her.

When the girls were tucked in bed, I sat down with my mom and told her about our unsuccessful search. Then she told *me* some news.

"Caroline called. The police think Harry Kuhn may be in Mexico, believe it or not."

Mexico! "Is Jake with him?" I asked.

"They don't know," she said. "They're trying to track him down, but it may take a while. I guess he's out in the country where there aren't any phones."

I felt like crying. I'd been searching every nook and cranny of my own little town — and Jake might be thousands of miles away. Would we ever find him?

CHAPTER 10

"Hi, Bart? It's me, Kristy," I said into the phone later that evening. "Could you — I mean, would you like to — um, why don't you come over for a little while?" I was having a hard time issuing the invitation. But I felt I *needed* to be with Bart for awhile. He'd been with me when I last saw Jake. He knew how worried I was and he was worried, too. I just didn't want him to think that I was *dependent* on him or something.

"Sure, Kristy," said Bart. "I'd love to. I was hoping that you'd call."

I barely heard him since I was so tangled up in my own feelings. But finally his words registered. "You would? You were?" I said. "Well, great. Come over whenever you can." I knew we wouldn't have much time to ourselves, since everybody in my family was home that night, including Karen and Andrew, who had arrived for the weekend. But

I figured it would be good to see him, anyway.

Bart showed up about forty-five minutes later. I was in my room, trying to concentrate on my math homework, but I wasn't getting anywhere with it. All I could think about was Jake. Where was he? Who was he with? Was he safe?

"Kristy!" my mom called from the bottom of the stairs. "Bart's here."

I threw down my pencil, glad to give up on trying to figure out what "X" equaled. And when I got downstairs and saw Bart waiting for me in the hall, I felt great. I realized that calling him had been the right thing to do.

"How *are* you?" he asked, putting his arm around my shoulders and giving me a little squeeze. It wasn't exactly a hug, since my mother and Karen were standing right there, but it made me feel as if he cared about me.

"I'm okay," I said. "I mean, I'm not *really* okay, but I'm okay, you know?" I blushed. I was babbling.

"I know," he said, smiling. "I know exactly what you mean. I feel the same way."

"Let's go into the den," I said. "We can put on some tapes and hang out for a while." I led the way, detouring through the kitchen to pick up some pretzels and pour us each a Coke.

I turned on some music — nothing too loud,

but nothing too mushy and romantic, either. Then I sat on the couch with Bart. "It still seems so unreal, doesn't it?" I asked. "I mean, that Jake is missing."

"It does," he said. "It's been over twenty-four hours now, though. I can't believe all that time has gone by since we last saw him."

We were both quiet for a minute, and I was sure Bart was thinking the same thing I was, how Jake had waved good-bye and trotted toward home, and how we had turned our backs and set off in the opposite direction.

"Do — do you feel guilty at all?" I asked Bart. "I mean, not that you *should* or anything. It's just that I do, a little."

"I do, too," he said quietly. "I keep thinking that if only we had insisted on walking him home — "

"He'd be there now!" I cried. "Safe in his bed."

The tape came to an end, and the room was suddenly very quiet. For a second (maybe a nanosecond) I wondered if Bart and I had run out of things to say to each other. I never thought *that* would happen. But then I realized that we were just having a hard time talking, because there wasn't anything to *say* about the situation. Jake was missing. We hadn't found him yet. We both felt upset and guilty. What was there to discuss?

I flipped the tape over, then sat down again and grabbed a pretzel. "You know — " I started.

"I keep — " said Bart at the same time.

We both laughed. "Go on," I said.

"No, you."

"Oh, nothing. I was just trying to figure out if there was anything else we could do. What do people *do* when someone's missing?"

Bart shook his head. "I don't know," he said. "They search for the person, but we've already done that." He sat quietly for a moment.

"What were you going to say before?" I asked.

"Oh, just that I keep thinking about how I would feel if it were one of the kids on *my* team who was missing," he said. "I feel so responsible for all of them, you know?" He looked at me. "What am I asking *you* for? Of course you know."

I sighed. "You know, whatever happened to Jake, whether he's lost or whether his dad took him, this experience must be really hard on him. I mean, imagine being kidnapped by your own father! What a mess." I thought of Jake, and about how scared or confused — or both — he must be. And before I knew it, my eyes had filled up with tears and one of them had spilled over. I could have died! I *never* cry in front of anyone. That's Mary Anne's thing, crying. But I'm different. I'm Kristy. I'm tough.

I reached up to wipe the tear away, but Bart got there first. His touch was gentle as he dried the tear. Then he kept his hand on my cheek as he looked into my eyes. "Kristy," he said. "It's going to be okay." He leaned toward me. I closed my eyes.

"Hey, you guys!" yelled Karen as she slammed the door open and ran into the den. "Jake's on TV!"

My eyes popped open. "Jake!" I cried. "Jake's on TV? You mean they found him?" I sat up straight.

"No," said Karen. "Just his *picture* is on TV. They're talking about how he's missing." She leaned down and turned on the TV in the den. "See?"

Jake's face filled the screen. I felt my stomach tighten when I saw his brown eyes. I recognized the picture that was being shown. It was Jake's school picture, which I'd last seen hanging on the wall in the Kuhns' front hall. The TV people had superimposed the word MISSING, in red, over his chest.

As we watched, the picture of Jake was replaced by a shot of Mrs. Kuhn, who was being interviewed by a local newswoman.

"Have there been any new developments in your son's case?" she asked. She was dressed in a trench coat. She held the mike up to Mrs. Kuhn's mouth.

"Not really," said Mrs. Kuhn. "We are still trying to locate my ex-husband in hopes that he may know where Jake is."

Obviously, she didn't want to say on the air that she suspected Mr. Kuhn might have *taken* Jake. The newscaster thanked her and was about to turn away, when Mrs. Kuhn stepped forward and started to speak quickly.

"I just want to ask anyone who has *any* information about my son to please call me," she said. "And Jake, if you can see me, wherever you are, I love you and I miss you, and I know I'll see you soon." Mrs. Kuhn looked so unhappy and so worried. I felt my eyes fill with tears again, but this time I held them back.

"She sounds kind of hopeful about seeing Jake soon," said Bart when the interview ended and a commercial came on.

"She does, doesn't she?" I answered. "I wonder if she knows something she doesn't want to tell the public yet."

Just then, the phone rang. I grabbed the extension. "Hello?" I said.

"Kristy? This is Caroline Kuhn." It was strange to hear her voice over the phone, when I'd just been watching her on TV. "I just wanted to let you know that things are looking up. We searched Jake's room about an hour ago, and I found some letters from Harry. In them, he talks about this woman — a friend of his that Jake apparently has met."

She didn't sound at all jealous about the woman. I wondered why she wasn't bothered that Mr. Kuhn had a "friend" already.

"Anyway," she went on, "the police seem to think she's a great lead. They're trying to call her right now, because she may know where Harry is."

"Great!" I said. Mrs. Kuhn sounded so optimistic. Her hopefulness was catching. She said she'd call as soon as she heard anything, and we hung up.

"What's happening?" asked Bart.

I filled him in. "Oh, Bart," I said after I'd told him about the new lead. "Something tells me Jake is going to be found really, really soon, and that he's safe and sound. I just *know* it."

"I hope you're right, Kristy," said Bart, smiling. "That would make a lot of people happy."

But an hour later, while Bart and I were watching a rerun of *The Brady Bunch*, Mrs. Kuhn called back. In a tired voice, she told me that the Dallas police had located the woman and questioned her, and that the woman had no idea where Mr. Kuhn was.

Bart left soon after, and I went to bed feeling as if I'd been riding a roller coaster all day, up and down, up and down. But the ride was no fun; all I wanted was to be back on solid ground. And that meant finding Jake.

CHAPTER 11

Friday

Jell-O, Jell-O, Jell-O. I hope I never see another Jell-O box again as long as I live. I have eaten lemon Jell-O, lime Jell-O, black cherry Jell-O, and strawberry Jell-O. I have made Jell-O with fruit salad in it, and Jell-O with pineapple rings. I thought Jell-O would be easy. I thought Jell-O was one thing nobody could mess up. But I was wrong. Luckily, though, my job at the Barretts' gave me a chance to have my "Jell-O breakthrough."

Mary Anne was almost ready to give up on home ec and resign herself to a failing grade. For some reason, maybe because she was so nervous, she couldn't do anything right in that class. She lost her notes. She left the stove burners on. She spilled things. When she was sewing her skirt, she accidentally attached it to the dress she was wearing that day, and didn't realize it until the bell rang. (She had to get a late pass to go to her next class.)

Mary Anne was not a happy homemaker.

"I *know* I can do it," she had said to me at lunch that day at school. "I just have to relax and have fun with home ec. But Mrs. Ploof makes me so nervous. She wants everything to be just so. When we had our table-setting test? She actually whipped out a tape measure to check that each plate was *exactly* one inch from the edge of the table. I mean, really!"

I sympathized with Mary Anne, honest I did. I've never been any good at that home-ec stuff, myself. And any other time I would have been glad to help her figure out ways to pull up her grade. But my mind was on only one thing lately: finding Jake.

Mary Anne was worried about Jake, too. She said she'd had trouble sleeping. She lay awake at night thinking of all the places he could be, all the things that could have happened to him. This was one time when having a good imagination was *not* helpful.

Anyway, I hate to admit it, but Mary Anne's home-ec problem was really kind of funny. It made me smile to think about her class having to *drink* the raspberry Jell-O she'd made because it never set. And I almost laughed when I thought about how one of the boys in her class, Pete Black, had said that another Jell-O mold she'd made would make a great weapon, since it was so hard. During study hall, he'd shown me a drawing he'd made of an AJL: an Automated Jell-O Launcher. It looked very high-tech.

Home ec was a nice distraction from worrying about Jake. Nice for me, that is. For Mary Anne, it was a practically a nightmare.

On the evening of the "Jell-O breakthrough," she'd put aside her worries (about her class and about Jake) in order to sit for the Barrett kids. Mrs. Barrett was going over to the Kuhns' house to keep Mrs. Kuhn company while the search for Jake continued. She was ready to leave when Mary Anne arrived. And even though she was only going over to a neighbor's house for the evening, she looked, as Mary Anne told me later, "as glamorous as always." Mrs. Barrett is really gorgeous. She could be a model: she has long, curly, chestnut hair, and a great figure, and she's always wearing these very elegant-looking outfits. She's one of those people who *never* runs her stockings or spills tomato sauce on her blouse.

Before she left, she told Mary Anne that the kids were "a little upset" about Jake. She said Buddy and Suzi were old enough to understand what was going on, and that it was affecting them. And Marnie, the baby, was picking up on *their* feelings and was just generally cranky.

Mary Anne assured Mrs. Barrett that she would do her best to keep things calm. But about two seconds after Mrs. Barrett walked out the door, all three kids exploded into action. Marnie screwed up her big blue eyes and started to wail—and like any two-year-old, she can wail loud enough to make you wish you were in another county. Then Buddy, who's eight, came running into the living room (where Mary Anne was busily trying to distract Marnie), shouting that Suzi had "totally ruined" the diorama he was making for school. It was for a book report, he said. It was supposed to be the farm where Charlotte and Wilbur lived, from *Charlotte's Web*. And Suzi kept trying to put her Little Ponies into the barn.

"Horses need a place to sleep," explained Suzi, who's five. She had run into the room behind Buddy. "If they stay out in the fields at night they might get horse-napped."

"Nobody's going to horse-nap your dumb pink pony," said Buddy. "Just keep out of my stuff, okay?"

Mary Anne, holding Marnie on her lap, was looking from one kid to another, trying to figure out how to make peace. She told me later that she must have been feeling kind of desperate, because the only thing she could think of was a cooking project. She suggested they make Jell-O.

"Jell-O!" said Buddy. "My favorite. Can we make lime? I like the green kind because it looks like slime."

"I like strawberry," said Suzi. "It's prettier."

"We'll make both," said Mary Anne, hoping that the Barretts' cupboards were stocked. She led the kids into the kitchen, where she found several boxes of Jell-O. Luckily, there were a couple of boxes each of lime *and* strawberry. Mary Anne put on some water to boil and reached for a bowl. Several cookie cutters fell out of the cabinet and she tried to stuff them back in. Then, she suddenly had a brainstorm. What if she made the Jell-O extra strong and poured it into a long, shallow baking pan? It would probably come out hard — she knew that from her home-ec "experiments." And then the kids could cut out shapes with the cookie cutters. It seemed like a perfect activity.

She prepared the Jell-O, poured it out, and put the pan into the fridge. She figured it would be ready to cut in a couple of hours.

"Suzi, while we're waiting for the Jell-O, why don't you bring your horses down here and we'll make them a barn of their own," she said. "And Buddy, why don't you bring your diorama downstairs so I can see it? *Charlotte's Web* is one of my favorite books."

Suzi and Buddy ran to get their stuff. Mary Anne sighed with relief. At least the older kids had stopped fighting. But Marnie had started to cry again, loudly. Mary Anne looked around for something to distract her with, and her eyes lit on a rattle shaped like a clown that had been left partway under the couch. Mary Anne scooted over to the clown and grabbed it without putting Marnie down. She waved the clown at Marnie. "See?" she said, "see the happy clown? Can *you* smile like that?"

Marnie didn't actually smile, but she did stop screaming as she held out her hands for the clown. Just as she settled down to play with it, Buddy and Suzi charged back into the room. Suzi was waving her toy horse, which was bright pink with a flowing purple mane, and Buddy was carrying his diorama, which fit inside a shoebox.

"See?" said Buddy excitedly. "There's the

web, and there's the place where Wilbur sleeps, and — "

"Shhh . . ." said Mary Anne. "Let's use *indoor* voices, okay?"

" — and there's the hatchet that Fern's dad was going to use to chop Wilbur's head off," Buddy went on, in a slightly quieter voice.

"Oh, ick, Buddy," said Suzi. "Why do you have to have *that* in there?"

"Because it's part of the story," explained Buddy patiently. "Dummy," he added under his breath.

"Buddy," Mary Anne said in a warning tone.

He looked innocently at her. "What?" he asked. "What?"

"*You* know," she said. "Don't call your sister names."

"Okay," he said. "But she is a — "

Mary Anne held up a finger. "Don't say it, Buddy."

He shut his mouth and turned to his diorama. "What could I use to make trees?" he wondered aloud.

"How about a green sponge?" asked Mary Anne. "I have one at home that you can use, if your parents don't have one."

Buddy bent to consider how sponge-trees would look.

"What about my pony barn?" asked Suzi, who had been waiting patiently for Mary Anne's attention.

"Right," said Mary Anne. "Okay. I saw an empty box in the kitchen. How about if we cut a door into it and draw windows and stuff on it with crayons?"

"Neat!" said Suzi. She ran to get the box. Soon both kids were busily cutting and drawing, and Mary Anne leaned back on the couch to catch her breath. Marnie had dozed off in a corner of the couch, and Mary Anne realized that she was probably cranky because she was exhausted.

Just as Mary Anne began to relax, Suzi looked up from her pony barn. "I think I'm going to sleep with my blanky tied to my arm tonight," she said, twirling one of her ponytails in her hand. "That way, if the kidnappers take me, I'll still have my blanky with me."

Mary Anne knows how kids feel about their security blankets, but this was a bit much. She figured that Suzi must be really scared.

"Do you think there are any kidnappers out tonight?" asked Buddy. Suddenly, he looked very vulnerable, crouched on the floor with his big knobby knees sticking out.

"No way," said Mary Anne. "Not around here, anyway." She realized that the kids had a lot of questions and a lot of fears, so she talked to them and tried to reassure them. She answered their questions, and told them that their parents were watching out for them and that they would be safe. Then, since it was almost time for bed, she decided to check out the Jell-O in the fridge.

"Hey, look!" she said to the kids, who had followed her into the kitchen. (Marnie had woken up by then.) "This worked really well." She shook the pan and the Jell-O hardly moved. Then she got out the cookie cutters and settled the kids at the kitchen table. They got the idea right away, and went to work. Soon they had made a plateful of shiny, jiggly stars, hearts, and Christmas trees. Mary Anne couldn't believe how well her recipe had worked.

After she'd put the kids to bed that night, with many comforting words about how safe they'd be while they were sleeping, Mary Anne went back downstairs and wrote up a description of the Jell-O treats she'd dreamt up. She was sure she'd be able to get extra home-ec credit for the idea. Maybe, she thought, she'd finally have a chance at passing the course. And it was all due to . . . Jell-O!

CHAPTER 12

"Jake! Jake! Jake!" I heard his name being called over and over. I tramped through thick underbrush, parting tree branches as I hunted for any sign of him. I kept thinking that if I just looked long enough, I would find him. Maybe he'd be behind that big bush over there, or maybe he was hidden in a little cave. I knew he couldn't be far. I knew I could find him. "Jake! Jake! Jake!"

I woke up with a start, and realized that I'd been dreaming. The voice calling "Jake" was my neighbor's dog, who likes to bark loudly in the morning.

I rolled over to look at my clock. It was eight-thirty, Saturday morning. I lay on my bed and stared at the ceiling. I did some quick figuring and realized that Jake had been missing for about forty hours. That was almost two full days. I swallowed, and felt the lump in my throat that had been there since Jake had disappeared. I still felt kind of guilty — and now I was also beginning to feel a little hopeless.

The police had been on the case from the beginning, and they were doing everything they could. I had mobilized the kids from school plus the kids from Jake's neighborhood, and we'd looked and looked, but we'd gotten nowhere.

Forty hours. If Jake had been kidnapped, he and his abductor must be pretty far away by now. And if he *hadn't* been kidnapped — it was almost too terrible to think about. Wherever he was, he could be hurt, or sick. And he was probably very hungry and thirsty. And definitely lonely and scared. Poor Jake.

When I first woke up, I felt so sad that I didn't even have the energy to get out of bed. But then I thought of Jake, hungry and afraid, and realized he needed people to help him, not to give up on him. I jumped out of bed and threw on the same clothes I'd left on my chair the night before. In the bathroom, I ran a brush through my hair and splashed water on my face. Then, for just a moment, I got distracted.

I leaned closer to the mirror to kind of check on what I would look like to someone who was about to kiss me. Oh, no! My nose looked *huge*! I tried leaning in at a different angle, and closing my eyes slightly. That was better, but

I still looked pretty weird, up close like that.

"Kristy!" yelled Karen from outside the bathroom door. She tried the knob, but luckily I'd put the lock on. "It's time for breakfast."

I jumped. Then I wiped the fog off the mirror, where I'd been breathing on it, and grabbed my toothbrush. "Just brushing my teeth, Karen," I yelled. "I'll be out in a minute."

As I brushed, my thoughts returned to Jake. I was almost hoping he *was* with his father. At least then he'd be safe, not hungry or scared. But it was still hard to imagine Mr. Kuhn abducting his own son. It was hard to imagine *any* father doing that — but I guess it does happen.

I headed downstairs for breakfast, deep in thought. Karen and Andrew were seated at the kitchen table, eating cereal. Emily Michelle was in her high chair, banging on her tray with a spoon. David Michael was hovering around Watson, who was cooking a pan full of sausages and eggs. I didn't see Charlie, but I knew he was probably still sleeping. He actually sleeps until *noon* some Saturdays! Sam was standing by the fridge, drinking milk right out of the carton. Luckily for him my mom wasn't in the room. She hates when he does that.

"Where's Mom?" I asked.

"She's outside checking on her daffodils,"

said Watson. "She was going to cut a bouquet to take to Caroline Kuhn."

I sat at the table and absentmindedly poured myself a bowl of cereal. As I ate, I thought some more about how it would feel to be kidnapped by your own father. What if *my* father had tried something like that?

I heard the screen door close, and looked up to see my mother walk into the kitchen with a huge bunch of daffodils in her hand. "Mrs. Kuhn's going to like those," I said.

"Think so?" my mother asked. "I know it's silly to think that *flowers* are going to help her feel any better about everything, but — "

"It's nice of you to think of her," said Watson. "Now, how about some eggs?"

My mother sat at the table with me and the other kids.

"Mom?" I said. "Do you know exactly where my father is right now? I mean, besides California?"

You might think that's a pretty weird question for a daughter to ask — and I guess it is. But I'm used to the fact that my father has almost nothing to do with me. It's only when I start to think about it that the situation seems strange.

"Well," she said. "I think David Michael got a birthday card this year from Petaluma."

"What does he *do* out there?" I asked. "Does

he have other kids? Why doesn't he write to us?"

All of a sudden I was curious about *everything*.

My mother gave a little laugh. "Well, let's see. Something with horses. Not that I know of; I doubt it. And, I don't know. There are all your answers, in order."

I thought about that for a moment. "Why do you doubt that he has other kids?" I asked.

"Well, because he wasn't very interested in being a family man," said my mother. "He hated the responsibilities that went with being a father."

"But did he love *us*?" I asked.

"Of course he did," she said. "How could anybody resist you?"

"I guess he never wanted custody of us," I said. "Did he ever even ask for, like, visitation rights?"

My mother shook her head. "I think it would have been hard for him to face you," she said. "After the way he left. It was so sudden, and so final. He just wanted out."

I tried to imagine the scene. "Do you think he ever thinks about us now?" I asked.

"Well, he does send you birthday cards," said my mother.

"Right," I said. "Like every third year, when he happens to remember."

"I'm sure he thinks about you," said my

mother. "And I'm sure he'd be proud to see how you've all grown up."

"Especially me!" said David Michael, who had been listening intently. "I was only a little baby when he went away."

"That's right," said my mom.

David Michael was quiet for a moment. He looked kind of worried. "Do you think he might kidnap me, just so he could see what I'm like now?" he asked.

My mom knows that you should always respect children's fears, so she didn't laugh. "No, I don't think he would," she said seriously. "He lives very far away, and he has another life now."

"What if somebody *else* tries to kidnap me?" asked David Michael. Apparently he'd been worrying about this.

"Yeah," said Karen, who has a *very* active imagination. "What if some mean guys grab us and take us away in their car?"

Andrew's eyes grew big and round. Then he started to cry.

"Whoa," said Watson. "It sounds as if you're all feeling a little scared because Jake is missing. Why don't we talk about it?"

"Good idea," said my mom. "First of all, does everybody know the rules about how to act when you're on your own, without an adult?"

Karen raised her hand as if she were in school. "Don't talk to strangers,"she said.

"Good," my mother said. "Except that, if you're in *trouble*, there are certain strangers that it's probably a *good* idea to talk to. Like police officers, or crossing guards. What else?"

"Always check with you or Daddy before we go anywhere, even if we're going with another grown-up," said Karen.

"Right," said Watson.

I couldn't help thinking that if Jake's dad *had* taken him, that rule would have saved everybody a whole lot of worry. Jake would have insisted on telling his mom where he was going.

"But what if somebody just *grabs* you?" asked Karen.

"If that happens," said my mother, "what you can do is make a big fuss. Yell and scream. Shout out that the person is *not* your mother or father. Don't be polite!"

"I can't believe you're telling us not to be polite," said Karen, grinning.

"Well, if you want to be safe, you can't always be polite," I said. I've read a lot about how children can be more safety-conscious. I figure that knowing that stuff is part of being a good baby-sitter. "I mean, it's polite to do what adults tell you to do, and to smile and answer their questions, but if the adults are complete strangers, you don't have to listen to them."

"Right," said my mom. "The thing to do is just be alert, and *think* about taking care of yourself. If a car pulls up and somebody asks you directions, you can give them, but stay a safe distance away from the car. Just be sensible, that's all."

"Also," said Watson, "it's a good idea to know where safe places are. If you're feeling scared, you might not be close to home. But you can go into a store, or the post office, or the police station, or the library. You can talk to the adults there about your fears."

Karen, Andrew, and David Michael all looked pretty solemn. They had been listening and paying attention to everything we said. A knock at the front door broke the tension, and Karen ran to answer it.

"It's Bart, Kristy," she called. "I can see him through the window."

"If it's Bart, I guess it's safe to open the door," I said, smiling.

Bart came in and sat at the table for a few minutes, talking with my mom and Watson. Then he and I and all the kids except Emily Michelle set out for the elementary school. Everyone who had searched the day before had agreed to come back and try again.

Karen and Andrew stuck near me and Bart

as we broke the searchers into groups. Matt and Haley Braddock joined me again, too. Matt, Haley told us, had remembered some other "favorite places" of Jake's — places where he went when he wanted to think. As soon as we were ready, we headed for the first one, which was in the woods behind the school.

CHAPTER 13

"Matt says there's a little clearing back here," said Haley. We were following Matt as he walked down a path through the woods. "He says Jake took him there once and made him promise never to show anyone else. But now he thinks he better break his promise."

I nodded. "Finding Jake is the most important thing right now," I said. "I'm sure he wouldn't be mad at Matt for bringing us there." As I walked, I kept stumbling over roots and getting stung by branches that hung over the path. I held one of them up so that Karen, Andrew, and David Michael could walk under it. Then, as Bart followed them up, I made sure he'd gotten hold of it before I let it go.

"Jake!" Bart was calling. "Jake!"

It was just like my dream. The woods were kind of pretty, with sunlight dappling the ground and green, green everywhere. It could have been a fun place for a picnic or a hike. But we weren't there for a picnic. We were there to look for Jake. "Jake!" I called. "Jake!" My throat was still sore from calling his name for hours the day before.

Up ahead, Matt had come to a stop. "This is it," he signed, once we had come into the little clearing. "But no Jake."

I didn't have to wait for Haley to interpret. I'd learned the signs for "no Jake" yesterday.

"I can see why he liked it here," I said. "I — I mean, why he *likes* it." I didn't want to start talking about Jake as if he were gone forever. The clearing *was* a pretty spot. There was a dead tree lying on its side; it made a good seat. Being in the clearing almost felt like being in a little room — just the right size for one person — except that instead of being in a house, it was outdoors. It was a great place but there was no sign of Jake. No sneaker prints, nothing.

Matt had looked discouraged when we first arrived in the clearing, but within a few minutes his spirit was back. He began to sign to Haley.

"He says there's this clubhouse in a meadow near here. We can follow the path until we come to it. Usually some older kids use it, but once in a while Jake and Matt go there if it's empty."

I looked at Bart and we both nodded. "Sounds good," I said. "Let's go."

We headed down the path again, single file. First Matt, then Haley. Karen and Andrew came next, with David Michael behind them. I was following David Michael, and Bart was following me. We were all calling as we walked. Once in a while I'd stop short, just to listen for a moment in case Jake himself was calling for help. But I never heard anything except our own voices.

After a while, the path led out of the woods and into a big, wide meadow. Wildflowers were blooming, and birds were swooping through the air. "Wow," I said. "This is beautiful. I've never been here before."

Bart took my hand as we walked down the path toward a tumbledown building that stood in the middle of the field. "The police have probably already checked this place," he said to me quietly.

"I know," I said. "But what does it hurt to check it again? The police could have missed a clue or something."

As we walked up to the clubhouse, a high-school-age guy came out of its door. "What do you want?" he demanded. "This is private property."

"It is not!" said Haley. "This field belongs to the town. My dad said so."

"Yeah, but we built this place," said another boy, who had come out behind the first one. "It's ours. Get lost."

"Hey, take it easy," said Bart. "We're not here to bug you. We're just looking for a missing kid. Jake Kuhn. Have you seen a little boy around here?"

I was proud of Bart. Those older boys were being pretty nasty, but he didn't get scared off.

"Jake Kuhn," said one of the boys. "I saw his picture on TV last night. You're friends of his?"

We nodded.

"I haven't seen him," the boy said. "But we can help look. How about if we check the underpass? You know, where the railroad tracks go under the road?"

I smiled at him. "I think the police have already looked there," I said. "But if you know your way around it, that would be great. Maybe they missed something."

"We could also check that old abandoned gas station," said the other boy. "I remember hiding there once when I was a little kid."

The boys loped off across the field. Bart and I grinned. "I'm glad *they're* checking out those places," I said. "I get the creeps near that underpass. And the gas station is pretty scary, too. All those old, broken-down cars." I turned to Matt. "Where should we go next?" I asked him.

He made a quick sign.

"Jugtown," explained Haley. "That store Matt and Jake go to all the time to buy baseball cards."

"Good idea," said Bart. "Maybe the owner saw Jake that afternoon."

We walked through the field until we came out on a street near the elementary school. There's a convenience store that Mary Anne and Claudia and I used to go to almost every day when we were little. It's been through several different owners since then, but it still looks the same.

A bell rang as Haley pushed the door open. We crowded in behind her, and I noticed right away that the store also *smelled* the way it used to. I took a deep breath, remembering what it felt like to come into that store with fifty cents in my pocket. I used to feel so rich — as if I could buy anything I wanted. Of course, back then all I ever wanted was a Chunky bar or a bag of potato chips. So fifty cents was enough. Fifty cents doesn't get me too far anymore, though. It barely pays the tax on a CD.

Suddenly I was feeling kind of grown-up.

"What can I do for you kids?" asked the man behind the counter. He seemed to lump us all together, and right away I felt pretty young again. I stepped out in front of the group and explained why we'd come. "So, we were wondering if maybe you'd seen him that day," I finished, after I'd described Jake.

The man shook his head. "Afraid I didn't," he said. "I wasn't even here on Thursday. My nephew was working. I'll ask him about it as soon as I get a chance." He shook his head. "It's a pity," he said. "I sure hope you find him soon. Jake's a good boy. And you're good friends, to be spending your Saturday searching for him." He looked at the counter in front of him. "Why don't you each take one of these?" he said, holding out a display box of miniature Reese's cups. "On the house. It'll help keep your energy up."

"Thanks!" I said. "Okay, kids, one each. And say thank you." I watched as each of the kids took a candy and thanked the man. "Thanks a lot," I said again as I took my piece. We headed out the door.

"Nice guy," said Bart.

"I know," I replied. "Too bad he hadn't seen Jake." We ambled along the sidewalk for a while. My feet were starting to hurt, and I could tell that the younger kids were getting tired.

Suddenly, two little white dogs started to bark at us from a fenced-in yard we were passing. "Hey!" called a woman. She stood up from weeding her flower bed and walked over to the fence. "Are you looking for that missing kid?" she asked.

"Yes!" I said. "Why? Have you seen him?" I felt excited all of a sudden. Maybe we were about to find Jake! Maybe this woman had seen him!

"No," she said. "Not for a few days. But before that, I saw him every day when he walked past here. A nice boy. My dogs love him."

Oh, well. It was just another bump on the roller coaster, after all. I tried not to let my feelings show, even though I was really disappointed.

"Good luck," the woman said. "Hope you find him."

"Thanks." Suddenly I was almost too tired to walk.

"Maybe we should call it quits for the morning," said Bart. "We can try some more after lunch."

I nodded, but just then Haley tugged on my sleeve. "Matt wants to check one more place," she said. "That place where they're building houses. He says Jake likes to get scraps of lumber and stuff there."

I shook my head. "I think it's a waste of time, Haley," I said. "That place isn't even on his way home from the softball field. It's in the opposite direction, on the way to *my* house."

Matt had seen me shake my head, and he started signing again right away.

"He really thinks we should look," said Haley. "Just this one last place, and then he doesn't have any more ideas."

I shrugged. "Okay," I said. "I'll try anything at this point." We turned around and headed in the opposite direction, toward the construction site. Everybody was getting tired. Karen started to whine, so I gave her a piggyback ride. Bart gave Andrew one, too.

"There it is!" said David Michael, pointing across the street.

We stepped off the sidewalk and walked across the lumpy, muddy lot. Bart paused for a second to look at a tractor, but I kept on walking toward the one house that was almost done. "Jake!" I called. My voice wasn't carrying very far anymore. "Jake!"

I stopped in front of a pile of lumber. I'd seen a scrap of cloth fluttering in the breeze. My stomach turned over. "Bart!" I yelled. "Come here — look at this." He ran to me. I pointed at the piece of fabric. "Isn't that the same color as the shirt Jake was wearing at our game?" I asked.

Bart nodded. "It is," he said. "Wow." He turned to glance at the rest of the construction site. "We'd better take a good look around."

I called the others. "Okay, kids," I said, when they had gathered near me. "Listen up. Everybody should be extra careful here, because this place could be dangerous. There could be nails on the ground, or open holes. But let's walk around a little and call for Jake."

They spread out and started to yell. I stayed where I was and listened as hard as I could. And then I heard it. A tiny, weak voice — calling for help.

CHAPTER 14

"Bart!" I yelled. "Come back here!" Bart came running. "Listen," I said, "do you hear something?"

We were quiet for a moment. Then Bart shook his head. "Nope," he said. "Do you think you heard something?"

"I'm almost sure of it. There was a voice — just a little, weak one — and it sounded as if it was calling for help. I just couldn't tell where it was coming from. Oh, Bart, do you think it could be Jake?"

He shrugged. "Let's listen again," he said. "First let's yell his name together and then we'll stop and listen. Maybe we'll be able to tell where the voice is coming from." He looked at me and crossed his fingers. "Okay, ready?" he said. "One, two, three — "

"JAKE!" we yelled. Then we stood as still as statues, hoping to hear a reply.

"I heard something!" said Bart. "Did you?"

I'd been holding my breath, and now I let it out. "I did," I said. "And I think it came from that direction." I pointed toward one of the half-built houses.

"That's what I thought, too," said Bart. "Let's go!"

We walked toward the house, stopping every few yards to call to Jake and to listen for a response. By then, the kids were following along behind us.

As we drew closer to the house, the voice we'd been hearing got a little louder, but it never sounded very strong. At one point I looked down and realized that my fists were clenched tight, out of nervousness, I guess. Could it really be Jake we were hearing? Were we really going to find him? I felt a little dizzy.

"Jake!" I called again. We'd reached the house, and I leaned into its skeletonlike frame and looked around. I didn't hear an answer. "I don't see anybody," I said to Bart. "But I could have sworn this is where the voice was coming from."

"Me, too," he answered. "How about if I stay here with the kids and listen while you explore inside the house. I'm sure he's nearby. We just have to pin down where he is." Bart was talking as if he were positive that it was

Jake we had been hearing. I couldn't let myself believe that yet. I was too afraid of being disappointed one more time.

"Okay," I said. I liked the fact that Bart was going to watch the kids while *I* did the exploring. A lot of boys would have insisted that it should be the other way around. I walked through the hole that would eventually be the front door. A floor had been laid, but it seemed temporary and not too solid. I walked carefully.

"Jake!" I called, every few steps. "Jake!" I headed into what would someday be the living room of the house. A space had been marked for a big picture window. I walked through that room and into what would probably be the kitchen. And then I saw the hole. In the floor was a dark, yawning hole. The basement! That's where the stairs to the basement were going to be — but they weren't there yet.

I ran to the hole. "Jake!" I yelled. "Are you down there?"

"Kristy? Is that you?"

I was shocked to hear my name. "YES!" I yelled. "Is that you, Jake?" My heart was beating a mile a minute.

"Uh huh," he answered.

"Jake, are you all right? Are you hurt? You must be hungry. How did you get down there?" I knew I was asking too many questions all at once, but I couldn't stop myself.

I heard him sniff, and I knew he was crying a little. "I'm pretty hungry," he said. "And my leg hurts a lot. Maybe it's broken." He sounded tired and scared.

"Oh, Jake," I said. "Listen, I'm going to leave you for a second, okay? Just to tell the others to get help. I'll be right back."

"Okay," he replied. Then, before I could even stand up, he called my name. "Kristy? I miss my mom. Can you make sure that she knows where I am?"

I felt my eyes tear up. What a good kid. He knew his mom was worried about him. "Of course. Anything else?"

"Could you get me something to eat?" he asked. "And I'm really thirsty, too."

"Food and drink, coming right up," I said. I jumped up and ran back to where Bart was waiting. "He's here!" I said. "In the basement. I can't figure out how to get him out, though. We'll need help. Somebody with a ladder."

"I'll go call the police," said Bart.

"And Mrs. Kuhn!" I said.

"And Mrs. Kuhn," he echoed. He took off across the building site, and I brought the rest of the kids into the house, after warning them to be very, very careful where they stepped.

"Jake!" I yelled into the hole. "You have some friends here, and they all want to say hello. Can you hear me all right?"

"I can hear you," said Jake weakly. "Who's up there?"

"Me!" shouted my brother. "It's me, David Michael. We've been looking for you for two whole days!"

"I'm glad you found me," said Jake.

"Hi, Jake!" said Karen. "Remember me? Karen? Are you okay?"

"Hi, Karen," said Jake. "I'm okay. I just wish it wasn't so dark down here. It's kind of scary."

"Ew!" she said. "It sounds yucky. Are there spiders?"

"I haven't seen any," said Jake.

"Hi, Jake," yelled Andrew. "It's Andrew, Karen's brother. Our stepsister Kristy is the one who found you. She kept looking and looking, and we looked with her."

"Lucky for me," said Jake. "Is anyone else with you?"

"Me — Haley — and Matt," said Haley. "He's going nuts because he can't sign to you. But I'll tell you what he's saying." She paused for a moment. "He says — he says he wants to know what you've been doing down there all this time. He's wondering if there's a rec room, with Nintendo and Ping-Pong and everything."

Jake laughed weakly, and the other kids laughed with him. "Right," he said. "I've been playing Super Mario Brothers the whole time."

I was glad to hear Jake laughing. Apparently, his spirits were okay, even if he did sound exhausted. "So, Jake," I said, "how did you end up down there, anyway?" I figured it was best to keep him talking until help arrived.

"It was dumb," he said. "See, I was on my way home after practice. But I remembered I've been wanting to check this place for used nails and screws. Me and Matt were going to start building a treehouse this weekend. Right, Matt?"

Haley had been interpreting for Matt as Jake spoke, and Matt nodded, smiling. "He remembers," said Haley.

"Anyway, I turned around and headed for this place," Jake continued, "but by the time I got here, it was pouring. All the workers were gone, so I figured I could get away with going into one of the houses, just to stay dry. I walked into this one, but I couldn't see too well. It was kind of dark because of the rain. I was feeling my way around, when all of a sudden — "

"You fell right through the floor!" I said. "I can see how that could happen. There's a giant hole here. The workers must be used to walking around it, but if you didn't see it, it would be easy to fall through."

"That's what happened," said Jake. "And then I couldn't get out! There aren't any stairs. The ceiling is about a million feet over my head. And anyway, even if there *were* stairs, I don't know if I could climb out. My leg is killing me." He started to cry again, quietly. I could tell he didn't want the other kids to hear him.

"But Jake, weren't the workers here yesterday?" I asked. "Didn't they hear you calling for help?"

"They were around," he said, "but they were running their machines all day, and I couldn't yell loud enough for them to hear. Plus, I kept falling asleep. I didn't get much sleep on Thursday night because my leg hurt, so by then I was really tired."

"Well," I said. "We're just glad we found you. Everybody's been so worried — "

Just then I heard brakes squeal outside, and a car door slammed. About two seconds later, Mrs. Kuhn appeared in the room. Bart was right behind her. "Where is he?" she asked wildly. "Where's Jake?"

I pointed into the hole.

"Oh, Jakey," she cried. "Are you all right, honey?"

"I'm okay, Mom," he said. "Really, I am."

He must have been so glad to hear his mother's voice.

Mrs. Kuhn started to cry. I put my hand on her arm. "He's okay," I said. "The police will have him out of there in no time."

"I know," she said, sobbing. "I'm just so relieved. Oh, Kristy, how can I ever thank you for finding him?"

I smiled and shook my head. I didn't need any thanks.

"Hey, Jake!" called Bart. I noticed that he was holding a brown paper bag, and now he tossed it down into the hole. "Your friend at the candy store sent you this."

A second later we heard Jake yelling happily, "Kit Kats! Twinkies! Doritos! Apple juice! All *right*!"

"This is one time I don't mind if he eats junk," said Mrs. Kuhn, wiping her eyes. "He can have whatever he wants. I'm just so happy he's safe!"

Bart told us that he'd gone to the convenience store to make his phone calls, and that the owner had insisted on filling up the bag for Jake. "He kept saying what a good boy Jake is," he told Mrs. Kuhn.

"Are the police coming?" I asked.

"Any minute," said Bart. "The rescue crew said they'd be right over." As he finished speaking, I heard sirens.

The crew got Jake out of the basement easily. All it took was a ladder, lowered into the hole. They brought him out on a stretcher. He was very dirty, and he looked tired and hungry, but he gave us a grin as he was carried out of the hole. A woman on the crew looked Jake over for broken bones and other injuries, while the rest of the workers pulled the ambulance around. "He's okay," she said. "Some bad bumps and bruises. The leg doesn't seem broken. But we'll take him to the hospital. He's probably dehydrated, and he needs to be checked more thoroughly."

By then, a crowd had gathered. A reporter from the newspaper was there, asking questions and taking notes. The local news team pointed cameras at the house. A lot of the other kids who had been looking for Jake had shown up, too.

As the ambulance pulled away with Jake and his mom inside it, the reporters pushed in to ask me and Bart questions. I pulled Matt beside me. "This is the guy you want to talk to," I said. "He's the one who knew just where to look."

CHAPTER 15

I pulled a dress out of my closet (it wasn't hard to choose one, since I only own about three) and walked over to the mirror. I held the dress up in front of me, to see how it looked. Not bad at all. I happen to like that dress — it's blue, with a drop waist and a full skirt — and I know I look pretty nice in it. I wore it once when my family went to a fancy restaurant to celebrate a promotion my mom had gotten at work.

I was trying to decide whether or not to wear the dress to Awards Night. It wasn't a big dress-up occasion or anything — lots of kids would be wearing regular school clothes — but for some reason I was feeling the urge to look a little bit special. I turned this way and that, imagining my hair up in a French braid and a strand of pearls (fake ones, of course!) around my neck. I imagined my friends complimenting me on how I looked. I imagined

Bart gazing at me with a special look in his eyes. And I was just about ready to put the dress on when suddenly I remembered some of the other things that are involved when you wear a dress.

A slip. Pantyhose. Shoes that pinch.

"Forget it," I said out loud. I practically *threw* the dress back into the closet and headed for my dresser drawers, where I knew I could find something a little more comfortable, a little more informal, a little more Kristy.

I decided on my best jeans and a new sweater, and I wore loafers instead of running shoes. I did *not* wear my favorite baseball cap, the one with a picture of a collie on it. (The collie reminds me of Louie, a dog we used to have.) But I didn't put my hair up, either. I wanted to be myself for Awards Night. After all, I was probably just going to be sitting in the audience, anyway. I didn't expect to get any of those silly awards they hand out. But it sure was going to be fun to watch some of the other kids get theirs. I had heard a rumor that Pete Black, who happens to be president of our class, was going to be named "Class Clown," and that he was planning to wear a clown suit for the occasion.

I heard the doorbell ring downstairs, and a minute later my mom yelled up to me that Bart was there. I'd invited him to Awards

Night as my guest, since he doesn't go to SMS. (He goes to Stoneybrook Day School, which is a private school.) I was glad that the student committee had decided to let each eighth-grader bring a guest, because that meant not only that Bart could come, but that Jessi and Mallory could be there, too.

I walked into the kitchen and found Bart there talking to my mom and Watson. "Hi, Bart. Boy, you look nice!" I blurted it out before I had time to think about how it would sound.

Bart blushed, which actually made him look even nicer. He was wearing a white button-down shirt, kind of baggy and cool-looking, and a pair of bleached-out jeans that fit him perfectly. "You look nice, too," he said. "But you *always* look nice."

I guess Bart really is the perfect boy for me — if I *have* to have a boyfriend. Not too many guys would think I "always look nice" — not in the outfits I usually run around in. But Bart doesn't seem to care much about clothes and stuff. He could tell you how many bases my team stole in the last game we played, but I'm sure he wouldn't remember which of my baseball hats I'd been wearing.

I checked my watch. "Ready to go?" I asked. "We're going to be late if we don't leave soon."

Charlie drove us to the school, and as soon as we pulled up I saw the other members standing in front of the auditorium, where we'd agreed to meet. Everybody looked great. Claud was wearing some kind of black jumpsuit-thing with a wide red belt. She looked incredibly cool, and so did Stacey, who was wearing tie-dyed leggings and a short dress that was kind of also like a man's shirt. (Sorry, I'm not so good at describing clothes!) I was glad to see that nobody was *really* dressed up. Dawn, Jessi, and Mal were just wearing jeans, and Mary Anne, who was talking to Logan, was wearing the skirt she'd finally finished making in home ec.

"Hey, the skirt looks great," I said. "Turn around, let's see."

"Kristy!" said Mary Anne. She was blushing. She is *so* shy. Sometimes I forget, and I embarrass her. But this time she smiled at me and gave a quick spin. "It came out okay, didn't it?" she said. "So did my final grade. Those Jell-O treats really did the trick. You know what's funny, though?" she said. "I thought I *invented* those things, but it turns out that the recipe for them is on almost every one of the new Jell-O boxes. They're called Jigglers. Isn't that a riot?"

I laughed. "Well, whatever they are, I'm sure I'll be making them sometime soon.

They're a great idea for a rainy-day project."

"Oh, wow, I almost forgot to ask," said Mary Anne. "But when you said 'rainy day,' it reminded me. How's Jake doing since he got home?"

"He's great!" I said. "In fact, he came to a Krushers' practice this afternoon. Patsy and Laurel were with him — they stick to him like glue these days. He looked shy at first, as if he wasn't sure the other kids would remember him or something. But they remembered him, that's for sure. As soon as he walked onto the field, everybody started applauding. The kids were so glad to see him."

"That's great," said Bart. "And he's feeling okay?"

"Oh, sure," I said. "He has a couple of bruises, and his leg's still sore, but he's fine. In fact, he pitched three innings today and he did a great job. He's our main relief pitcher from now on."

"We should plan another Bashers – Krushers game soon," said Bart. "Now that things are back to normal."

"There is one thing I'd like to know," said Mallory. She loves mysteries, and she never forgets a clue. "Where *was* Mr. Kuhn, anyway?"

I laughed. "He was in Mexico. He went on business. And before that he'd been in Texas."

"He was never here? What about that car that Patsy saw?" Jessi asked.

"I guess there must be another one that looks like Mr. Kuhn's," I said. "At least to Patsy. She misses her dad a lot. But she'll see him soon. He's going to be able to come to Jake's birthday party, after all."

"That's great," said Mary Anne. I noticed that she had tears in her eyes. Mary Anne just loves a happy ending.

"Hey, we better get inside," said Claudia. "It sounds as if they're about to start."

Sure enough, I could hear the microphone shrieking and popping as the AV crew tested it. We ran in and found a row of seats near the back. I sat down between Bart and Mary Anne, and waited for the program to begin. Mr. Kingbridge, the vice-principal of SMS, sat on the stage over to one side. He looked like he'd rather not be there, but I figured he had to be, just so there would be at least *one* adult at Awards Night. One of the AV guys spoke into the mike.

"Testing, testing," he said. "One, two, th — "

The mike shrieked loudly, and the boy jumped back. Mr. Kingbridge winced. Everybody in the audience broke up. The boy laughed along with them, and pretended to strangle the mike. "Let's try that again," he said.

Finally everything was ready. "Ladies and germs," said the AV guy, "may I introduce the president of the eighth grade, Mr. Pete Black — otherwise known as Bozo!"

Pete walked onstage dressed in a clown costume. He looked *ridiculous*! He had put on a big red nose, a wig the color of cotton candy, and these huge, gigantic shoes. Mary Anne and I looked at each other and cracked up. Everybody else was laughing, too.

"What?" asked Pete, acting as if nothing were unusual. Then he laughed, too. "Okay, we have a lot of awards to give out tonight, so let's get started," he said. "First, I'd like to introduce my assistant for this evening, Alan Gray."

Alan Gray, who is the most obnoxious boy in our class, came out of the wings. He was *also* dressed in a clown costume. Pete glared at him. "Hey, what's the idea?" he asked. The audience cracked up again.

"Don't be so sure you're going to win that Class Clown award," said Alan. He was holding one hand behind his back. "*I'm* going to win it. But there's another prize you might get — the *booby* prize!" He whipped a big pie out and shoved it in Pete's face.

The auditorium went wild. Mr. Kingbridge started to get up out of his seat, then sat down again. Pete looked shocked for a second, but then he laughed and wiped some of the whipped cream off his face. He tasted it and smiled. "Thanks for the pie, Alan," he said. "It's delicious." A girl walked out of the wings and gave Pete a towel.

"They planned that, didn't they?" I whispered to Mary Anne. She nodded, smiling.

Then Alan and Pete started handing out the awards. As it turned out, neither of them won the Class Clown award. The class had voted for this guy named Justin Forbes instead. Pete and Alan pretended to be mad, but no more pies were thrown.

Pete gave out some more awards, for stuff like Best Excuse For Not Doing Homework (a girl named Erica Blumberg won, for telling her teacher that her mom had composted her report), Most Often Seen Sleeping (this guy named Jerry won — he was always taking naps in study hall), and Worst Dresser (Mr. Kingbridge — as an "honorary eighth-grader" — won that one!). Then Pete announced that it was time for the academic awards. Guess what the first one was? "Most Improved Home-Ec Student." And guess who won?

Mary Anne made Logan go up to the stage with her to pick up her little plastic trophy. As Pete handed it to her, he said, "I guess this means that we won't be able to deploy the Jell-O Launcher after all." Mary Anne blushed so hard that I could see her red face from the back of the auditorium.

Finally all the awards had been given out. But Pete announced that there was one more award to present. "As you know, we try not to be serious on Awards Night," he said. "But just this once we're going to be. One of our classmates was responsible for doing something very special recently, and we'd like to acknowledge her for it. If she hadn't spent so much time organizing people and sticking to the search, a little boy might still be lost. Kristy Thomas, come and get your award!"

I was shocked. My friends were looking at me and grinning. I glanced at Bart, and he leaned over and kissed me — in front of everybody! "You're terrific, Kristy," he said. "Go on up there."

I walked to the stage, feeling like I was dreaming. I took the plaque from Alan, and stood there while everybody clapped. "Thank you," I said, finally. "This means a lot. But it's not just mine — I have to share it with everybody who helped with the search.

Thanks to them — and especially to a boy named Matt Braddock — Jake is home safe." I wiped my eyes and smiled. I guess Mary Anne's not the only one who loves a happy ending.

Look for Mystery #5

MARY ANNE AND THE
SECRET IN THE ATTIC

I skipped over the next five boxes I found, since they all had Sharon's handwriting on them. Then, behind an old broken table, I found a box with my dad's handwriting on it. "Miscellaneous," it said on top. I pulled it into the light and opened it up. Right on top, I saw an old photo album. "All right!" I said out loud.

I sat down right there with the album on my lap and started to look through it. The first pictures were from my parents' wedding. The one I liked best was an informal shot of the two of them walking toward the camera. My mom looks really happy, and my dad has this special smile on his face — he looks like someone with a wonderful secret.

The pictures looked familiar, and I realized that I'd seen them before. I kept leafing through that book, and then picked up another. Baby pictures! There I was, sitting in my dad's lap, smiling like a total goofball and wearing the dumbest little bonnet. I knew I'd never seen those pictures before — I'd have hidden them if I had, to prevent blackmail. I turned a few pages and watched myself get a little older. I still looked pretty goofy.

Then I saw some pictures that really confused me. In them, I was still really, really young. I was sitting on a porch I didn't recognize, with two older people I also didn't recognize. I was sure it was me, since I could see the little "Mary Anne" necklace that I always had around my neck. But who were those people? And where was that porch? There were other pictures, too: me and the two people sitting at a table, me and the two people under a tree. My hair was longer in some of the pictures, and my clothing was sometimes wintery and sometimes summery. Whoever those two people were, I'd spent quite a while with them. I looked closer at their faces — I even shone the flashlight on the pictures — but I couldn't figure out who they were.

Don't miss any of the latest books
in the Baby-sitters Club series
by Ann M. Martin

THE BABY-SITTERS CLUB®

by Ann M. Martin

The Baby-sitters' business is booming, and the fun never stops!
Don't miss out on any of it—collect them all!

More titles... ▶

The Baby-sitters Club titles continued...

Available wherever you buy books...or use this order form.

Scholastic Inc., P.O. Box 7502, 2931 E. McCarty Street, Jefferson City, MO 65102

Please send me the books I have checked above. I am enclosing $_____
(please add $2.00 to cover shipping and handling). Send check or money order - no cash or C.O.D.s please.

Name _____

Address _____

City_____ State/Zip _____

Please allow four to six weeks for delivery. Offer good in the U.S. only. Sorry, mail orders are not available to residents of Canada. Prices subject to change.